She Shifted, feeling her body slide into its familiar Fey form. Her body stretched and grew. Her tail and whiskers slid into her skin, her hair flowed down her back, her front paws became hands. She ended up in a sitting position, her knees drawn to her chest, the robe draped over her like a tent. Inwardly she sighed, and wished that there were a more dignified way of Shifting into clothes.

Then she slid her arms through the sleeves, and her head through the neck hole, letting the stiff fabric flow around her. It was a woman's garment, although she had no idea why someone would store one in a bank—or perhaps she did, and didn't want to think about illicit affairs among Nyeian bankers.

Solanda lifted her long hair out of the garment's neck, and let it fall down her back. Licia bit her lower lip, and the other Fey looked down. They hadn't realized they were talking to the best Shifter in the Black King's army—at least, not until now.

The Fey Series:

Destiny (A Short Novel)
The Sacrifice
The Changeling
The Rival
The Resistance
Victory
The Black Queen
The Black King

Destiny

A STORY OF THE FEY

><

KRISTINE KATHRYN RUSCH

*wmg*PUBLISHING

Destiny

Sacrifice

Destiny

A STORY OF THE FEY

Solanda walked the cobblestone streets of Nir, the capitol city of Nye, her tail up. She had a meeting with Rugar, the son of the Black King. He had sent a Wisp to find her, and it had taken the little creature nearly a day to do so.

Solanda was in her cat form, as she had been since the Fey captured this repressed country — and thus very difficult to find. The Nyeians had many faults — they were prissy, overdressed, and pasty faced, not to mention abominably poor soldiers — but they did treat their animals well. She had found a family who fed her to excess, allowed her to roam outside, and pampered her as no cat should be pampered.

How appalled they would be if they ever discovered the golden cat their daughter had adopted was really a Fey Shapeshifter.

Solanda's tail twitched once in amusement. Every day she imagined eating her lovely tuna dinner in the glass plate that the family gave her, and then Shifting into her Fey form just to say thank you.

She didn't know what would appall the Nyeians the most: the fact that she was Fey, or the fact that she would be naked. She doubted any of them had seen a naked woman before: the wife managed to change her clothing one piece at a time, without ever taking it all off at once, and the husband didn't seem to think this unusual. He would probably be more shocked than his wife at the appearance of a naked Fey woman in his house. He would probably fall over in a dead faint.

Only the daughter, a girl of five, was redeemable. Esmerelda was a good child. She had to be. She was raised Nyeian. Her mother trussed her in layers upon frothy layers of clothing, making movement nearly impossible, and then yelled at the poor child whenever she did something natural, like running.

Sometimes Solanda thought she went back to that household at night because she felt sorry for the child. But in truth, she stayed there because they gave her fish properly deboned and they brushed her, and they put a warm cedar bed in Esmerelda's room. Esmerelda, good child that she was, never confessed to her parents that she often picked up the cat and carried her to bed, cuddling with her long into the night.

And Solanda would never tell anyone — Fey or Nyeian — that sometimes she purred when she slept, pressed against the little girl's back.

Shifters were supposed to be the coldest of the Fey, the most fickle members of a warrior people, incapable of real emotion, flighty, restless and completely self-absorbed. They also were supposed to take on the characteristics of the animal they had chosen to Shift into, so

Solanda's fickleness — theoretically — was doubly compounded by the fact that she had chosen the cat as her alternate Shape.

Of course, it didn't matter how many times she had proven herself trustworthy. In the war against Nye, such as it was, she had done intelligence for the Black King. She had worn her cat form and slinked into Nyeian villages, soldiers' camps, and mess halls, keeping her ears open, and learning more than she should have.

Most countries that the Fey had fought had banned strange animals from military compounds. Solanda had heard that the Co had gone so far as to slaughter any strays, thinking they might be Fey reconnaissance. But the Nyeians had a fondness for cats, and while they kept stray dogs out of their camps, they fed cats on the side.

Solanda had spent most of the war the pampered resident of a Nyeian general's tent. He used to feed her bits of meat off his own plate while telling his staff his battle plans for the next day.

And then when he fell into his snoring sleep, she would go to the nearest Shadowlands and inform the Fey general of all she had heard. Toward the end of the war, she reported directly to the Black King, who shook his head at the stupidity of the Nyeians.

Conquering Nye was the first step toward world dominion. The Black King didn't say that, but Solanda knew that was his goal. The Fey were a great warrior people, but they only owned half the world right now. The Black King — and the Black Throne — wanted all of it.

Solanda entered the merchant sector of Nir, and silently cursed to herself. The merchants often shooed cats out of this area. Her presence here was suddenly noticeable, and she didn't dare Shift. She'd shock an entire community of Nyeians — which would probably be good for them.

Scents from the nearby vendor stalls caught her nose. Fried beef, more fish, some sort of vegetable something which turned her feline stomach. The fish was enticing. It almost made her forget that she was here because she had been summoned by the Black King's son.

Rugar had been her commander for part of the Nye campaign. He was an able warrior, frustrated under his father's tight leash. The problem with Rugar was that he believed himself to be the equal of his father, and he was not.

Solanda would rather work with the Black King, ruthless as he was, than with his less-talented son.

The tall stone buildings prevented the sun from getting to the cobblestone. The stone was wet beneath her paws from the morning rain. The air was thick and muggy, making the six layers of clothes the Nyeians wore look even more uncomfortable.

The handful of Fey who were on the street wore their traditional uniform — a leather jerkin and pants. The Fey were so much taller than the Nyeians that even if they didn't dress differently, they would be noticeable.

She ducked under some clothing stalls, past the buildings that housed the year-round indoor merchants, and turned on the street that led to the Bank of Nye. The Black King had taken over the building. It was four stories of gray stone, towering over the buildings around it — as close to a palace as there was in Nye.

She sighed heavily and crossed the street, climbing up the stone steps and staring at the large stone door. She'd have to Shift just to get into the place.

Then she saw a nearby window ledge. The window was open. She leaped onto the ledge and jumped to the stone floor inside. She thought this building unusually cold for a Nyeian structure. The house where she was pampered was made of wood, and had thick rugs on its floors. Every surface was soft, and the air perfumed.

Here the air smelled like chalk and the stone was chilly despite the heat. There were no guards in this room, although there should have been. It looked like it was someone's office — a desk in the center, chairs on the side for supplicants.

The door was open and led into a cavernous hallway. She heard voices and followed them. Several Fey guards huddled in an alcove. They were Infantry and young, tall even though they hadn't come into their magic yet. Their dark skin and black hair was a welcome sight. She'd gotten tired of looking at the pasty-faced Nyeians, and hadn't realized how much she missed her own kind.

"…fool's errand, don't you think?" One of the young men said.

"If it's so important, why doesn't the Black King go?" another asked.

"Blue Isle is important," said a young woman. "It's the only stop between here and Leut."

Leut was the continent on the other side of the Infrin Sea. The Black King wanted to go there more than anything. He wanted to conquer as much of the world as he could before he died.

"If we are going to conquer the world," the girl was saying, "we have to go through Blue Isle first."

"Then it doesn't make sense," the first man said. "Why send Rugar? He's not as good a commander as his father."

"Maybe," Solanda said in her most authoritative voice, "the best commander in the world has a plan that's too sophisticated for you to understand."

They all turned. They had similar upswept features, narrow faces, and pointed ears. Solanda had often thought that her people looked like foxes — most of them, anyway. Shifters, like her, often took some of the characteristics of their animals. Her hair and skin were more golden than dark, and she had the Shifter's mark on her chin — a birthmark that established who and what she was when she was in her Fey form.

But they couldn't tell now. All they could do was tell that a cat had spoken to them.

"Well," she said, sitting on her haunches and wrapping her tail around her paws. "Where do I start? Do I reprimand you for gossiping in the middle of the day? Do I tell you that I got into the building through a window that some careless fool left open and, if I had been some young Nyeian bent on assassination, I could have walked right past you and you wouldn't have noticed? Or do I ask that one of you poor, magickless fools get me a robe so that I can have my meeting with Rugar?"

They didn't answer her. She raised her chin slightly. Amazing how she could intimidate them, even though she was so very small.

"By the Powers," she snapped. "Get me a robe. And put a guard on the window."

She nodded over her head toward the room she had just come out of.

Two of the young men ran off toward the room. The third young man hurried off, presumably to get her a robe. That left the young woman.

"I really should report this," Solanda said. "Technically, you put the Black King's life in danger."

"From the Nyeians?" the young woman snorted. "You snarl at them and they run. They couldn't fight us in the war, and once they found out that they'd remain in charge of their businesses, they really didn't care that we took them over. Why would one of them try to get in here?"

"Revenge?" Solanda said. "We did, after all, slaughter half their army. Those young men were related to someone."

"Then that should take away half the threat, shouldn't it?" the young woman said. "After all, the Nyeians believe that only men are capable of fighting."

Solanda felt amused. "I have a hunch that belief has changed since they were defeated by us. What's your name?"

"Licia," the girl said.

"You haven't come into your magic yet, have you?"

The girl straightened her shoulder. Magic was always a touchy subject with Infantry. They were tall enough to show that they would get magic, but chances were if they neared adulthood and still hadn't come into their magic, their abilities would be slight.

"No," she said.

"You showed a tactician's mind. Why do you waste it gossiping with people who aren't worthy of you?"

The girl straightened her shoulders. "I don't normally guard. I am usually in the field."

"But there's no field at the moment, is there?" Solanda said. "What are you doing here?"

"Rugar asked me to come. He says his daughter needs more swordfighting training."

Solanda narrowed her eyes. Jewel, Rugar's middle child, was the most promising of all his raggedy offspring. She hadn't come into her magic yet either, but her height and her heritage suggested when her magic came it would be powerful. She was a good swordswoman now — Solanda had seen her fight in the last of the Nye campaign.

"Why would she need more training?"

Licia shrugged. "I suspect it has something to do with the fight Rugar had with his father this morning."

Solanda tilted her head to show her interest.

"They just left that room you came through. They were screaming at each other all morning long."

"About what?" Solanda asked, realizing that she was now gossiping. But she didn't want to go into a meeting with Rugar with less knowledge than he had.

"About going to Blue Isle. Rugar says he won't go without his daughter."

"Not his other children?"

"He didn't mention them." Then Licia smiled. "At least not at the top of his voice."

Solanda suppressed a sigh. The Black King favored Jewel. He felt that her brothers were idiots — and he was right. Their magic was slight, like their mother's had been. Rugar's entire life had been about defying his father. Rugar should have married a woman who had great magic. Instead, he had chosen someone he could control.

The young man returned with a flowing golden robe that was clearly of Nyeian origin. Solanda didn't ask where he had gotten it. She didn't thank him. Instead, she said, "Place it over me."

He did, blotting out the light. The robe smelled faintly of perfume and perspiration, but it clearly hadn't been worn in some time. The fabric was heavy satin — too heavy for a humid day like this — but she wasn't in the position to be choosy. If Rugar was planning something stupid, she wanted to meet him Fey to Fey. Psychologically, it gave her an advantage.

She Shifted, feeling her body slide into its familiar Fey form. Her body stretched and grew. Her tail and whiskers slid into her skin, her hair flowed down her back, her front paws became hands. She ended up in a sitting position, her knees drawn to her chest, the robe draped over her like a tent. Inwardly she sighed, and wished that there were a more dignified way of Shifting into clothes.

Then she slid her arms through the sleeves, and her head through the neck hole, letting the stiff fabric flow around her. It was a woman's garment, although she had no idea why someone would store one in a bank — or perhaps she did, and didn't want to think about illicit affairs among Nyeian bankers.

She lifted her long hair out of the garment's neck, and let it fall down her back. Licia bit her lower lip, and the other Fey looked down. They hadn't realized they were talking to the best Shifter in the Black King's army — at least, not until now.

Fools. Shifters were rare. How many of them would come into the Black King's dwelling and order Infantry around?

"Licia," she said, "announce me to Rugar."

The girl's skin colored slightly, but she moved in front of Solanda and led her down the hall. It got stuffier the farther in they went. Solanda was grateful that her feet were bare. The cool stone was going to keep her from melting in this robe.

Licia led her up a flight of stairs into a rabbit's warren of what had once been offices. Solanda smiled. Rugar was hidden here, in an obviously less desirable area of the building. The Black King had a thousand ways of showing his displeasure with everyone around him.

Licia knocked on a door at the end of the hall. Solanda stood far enough back that she wasn't visible from inside. She heard Rugar's gruff voice, and then Licia's response, announcing Solanda.

The door opened, and Licia stepped aside.

"I guess that means you're supposed to go in," she said.

Solanda stopped and put a hand on the girl's shoulder. She spoke softly so that Rugar couldn't hear. "If Rugar and his father are fighting," she said, "side with the old man. Rugar is not the future of this race. You're better off remaining in Nye with the Black King than going to Blue Isle with Rugar."

Licia nodded, then glanced over her shoulder as if she were afraid of Rugar. Solanda walked past her and through the open door.

Rugar stood in the center of the small room. He was medium height for a Fey, and his features had a predatory, hawk-like look to them. His almond-shaped eyes were the deep black that Solanda associated with the Black Family. It was as if the Throne echoed in their very essence. He had thin cruel lips, and an expression of permanent unhappiness.

For man in his fifties with grown children, he looked startlingly like a petulant child.

"You sent for me," she said, not disguising her lack of respect for him.

He clasped his hands behind his back, his father's favorite stance. "I'm taking an army to Blue Isle. You will be part of it."

She snorted. "I serve your father, not you."

Rugar glared at her. "He gave me permission to choose whomever I wanted from the standing armies in Nye."

"You have no need for a Shifter," she said. "Blue Isle is a tiny place, filled with religious fanatics who have never seen war. You'll sail in with your troops, wave a few swords, and be able to claim victory over an entire country in the space of a day. I'll be useless to you."

He shook his head. "I'm taking you, and a lot of Spies and Doppelgängers. I am to be military governor of Blue Isle. My father will launch an attack from there onto Leut."

Solanda narrowed her eyes and was glad she wasn't in cat form. She probably would have found an excuse to scratch Rugar, and that wouldn't have been good for either of them.

"Spies, Doppelgängers, and a Shifter," she said. "It sounds like an intelligence force. You won't need it if you conquer the country as quickly as you believe you will."

His gaze went flat. "I will need it."

She stared at him for a moment. He knew something and he wasn't going to share it with her. Spies made sense, even in an easily conquered country. They would find the pockets of resistance. But Doppelgängers had no place there. They killed their hosts and then took over the body, including the memories. Except for the gold flecks in the eyes, no one could tell them from their victims. Doppelgängers had a sophisticated magic — one that the best commanders used sparingly. And certainly didn't waste them on an already conquered country.

"You have no need for me," she repeated. "I stay with the Black King."

"You'll come with me."

"Your father said so?"

"No, but he will."

"Because he already acquiesced on Jewel?"

Rugar started. He hadn't expected her to know that.

Solanda raised her eyebrows and allowed herself a small smile. "I am good at gathering intelligence."

"And," he said, "as you pointed out, there's no need for intelligence gathering in a conquered country."

She nodded. "I'll go to Leut with your father, when he's ready. Until then, I'll relax here."

"Solanda —"

"Rugar," she said, holding up a hand. "You and I have no great liking for each other. I have a hunch your father is sending you to Blue Isle to get you out of his sight. I'd rather not be associated with you in any way. Right now, I hold your father's respect. I'd rather not change that."

Rugar took a step toward her. She could feel the violence shimmering in him.

She grabbed the doorknob. "Touch me," she said, "and I'll scratch out your eyes."

"You can't touch me. I'm a member of the Black Family."

She smiled. "I'm a Shifter. Unpredictable, irresponsible, flighty — remember? I'm sure the Powers would let this slide."

"But my father would not," Rugar said.

"Oh," Solanda said softly, "but I think he would."

2

She tried to see the Black King before she left the building, but he was nowhere to be found. His personal guards were gone as well. She decided she would find him in the morning, and went back to her life as a pampered Nyeian cat.

The home that she had chosen was a large one on the outskirts of Nir. It had two stories filled with more clutter than any home she had ever seen. Books of poetry, musical instruments, incredibly ugly paintings, and furniture everywhere. The only saving grace was that the furniture was comfortable and the kitchen had a cat door that she could escape through when the wife decided it was time for music.

Solanda slipped through the cat door, past the kitchen hearth. One of the three Nyeian servants was cleaning the pots from the evening meal. The air smelled faintly of roast beef, and Solanda's stomach rumbled.

Still, she didn't beg from the servant. She knew better. The idiot had kicked her "accidentally" once, and had the scars to prove it. But Solanda knew if she attacked anyone in the house too many times, she would be thrown out, and she wasn't willing to lose her rich dinners and soft bed just yet.

She blended into the hideous yellow wallpaper as she hurried up the stairs to Esmerelda's room.

Esmerelda sat on the edge of the bed, fingering a rip in her dress. She had a forlorn expression on her small face. Her brown hair hung limply around her cheeks, and a streak of dirt covered the pantaloons beneath the skirt.

Solanda had never seen Esmerelda look dirty before, nor had she seen the girl's hair loose at any time except bedtime.

"Oh, Goldie!" Esmerelda raised her voice in relief. She was speaking Nye, which was a language that Solanda hadn't known well when she moved into this house. Here her Nye had improved greatly, but she wanted to be fluent in it by the time she left.

The little girl launched herself off the bed and grabbed Solanda before Solanda could jump out of the way. Esmerelda wrapped her arms around Solanda and held tightly. Esmerelda had never done that before. If she had been a grabby little girl, Solanda would have been gone a long time ago.

So this meant, quite simply, that something was wrong.

Solanda let herself be held for a moment, then she turned her head toward the door and flattened her ears. Esmerelda, smart child that she was, understood both signals. She pushed the door closed, and then let Solanda go.

Solanda jumped on the windowsill. Esmerelda followed her, but didn't open the window like she usually did.

The room was hot and sticky. Solanda wouldn't be able to stay here too long if that window wasn't opened.

"I don't dare," Esmerelda said softly. "Mommy's really mad at me. She didn't even let me have dinner."

Now Solanda was interested, but she didn't want the story, not yet. She bumped her head against the window's bubbled glass.

Esmerelda bit her lower lip and shook her head.

Solanda placed a paw on the glass and meowed softly.

"Okay," Esmerelda whispered. "But if anyone comes, I'll have to close it."

Solanda almost nodded, then caught herself. When Esmerelda came close, Solanda bumped her affectionately with her head, and then watched as the little girl pulled the window open.

A cool breeze made its way inside. That was the other nice thing about this house. Esmerelda's room opened onto a large undeveloped area, so the smells of the outdoors came in strong. Breezes were unencumbered. Esmerelda's mother hated this, and often wished for close neighbors, but Solanda saw it for the blessing it was.

Esmerelda knelt down beside the window and put her elbows on the sill. She didn't touch Solanda, but she was still a bit too close. Her body heat was ruining the breeze.

"I been so bad," she said, "I won't get to go outside ever again."

Solanda watched her. The little girl had never been able to resist a cat's gaze. Solanda had never seen a child who was so very lonely. Esmerelda wasn't allowed to play — except with dolls whose clothing was frilly as the stuff she was trussed in — nor was she allowed to associate with the neighboring children who were, in her parents' mind, beneath her. She had lessons in poetry and music, art and dancing, but she liked none of it. What she really wanted to do was run as far as she could, and climb trees and learn how to swim.

She'd probably never get to achieve those goals.

"I was running this afternoon," Esmerelda said. Her face was wistful. She leaned her forehead against the glass. "Mommy was looking at fruit and I thought I could just go around the block, but she saw me. I guess she followed me."

Esmerelda had done this before, and it hadn't gotten her sent to bed with no supper. Solanda suspected the problem had something to do with the rip in the dress. Clothing was sacred, at least to this family. Solanda wanted to tear every piece so that this little girl could be free.

"She saw me fall." Esmerelda said, fingering her skirt. "She saw me hit a Fey."

Solanda stiffened. She almost asked who, and caught herself. Two near lapses in one conversation. She was getting much too relaxed with this child.

Esmerelda ran a soft hand over Solanda's head. Her touch was gentle again, as it had always been before.

"She said she was the Black King's granddaughter, and she yelled at Mommy for dressing me the way she did. And Mom yelled back. The lady said yelling at her was like yelling at all the Fey all at once."

Only one Fey woman could make that claim. Jewel. No wonder Esmerelda's mother was upset.

"And then Mommy told Daddy and he said that the Fey might hurt us. Because I ran." A tear coursed down Esmerelda's cheek.

And those fools were blaming the child for being a child. Solanda pushed against the girl's hand, and Esmerelda sniffled.

"I didn't mean to run. I just can't stay still sometimes."

Solanda understood that. She could never stay still. It was a curse of being a Shifter. It was the reason Fey wisdom said that Shifters were the most heartless of the Fey. Most Shifters did not have children, and most rarely stayed anywhere long enough to form a real relationship.

Esmerelda sighed. "I wish I was like you. I do what I want. Or like that Fey lady. She was nice to me. She didn't like Mommy though."

Neither did Solanda.

"She said children shouldn't be dressed like me. She said I ran into her because my clothing didn't let me run properly."

Probably true, Solanda thought.

"And that made Mommy really mad."

Esmerelda let her hand slide off Solanda's neck. She bunched her hands into fists and rested her chin on them, looking fierce and strong. Solanda felt her whiskers twitch in amusement. One day, Esmerelda's parents would no longer be able to control this child. If she was this strong, articulate, and intelligent at five, she would be impossible to control at fifteen.

Especially with all of the Fey influence around her.

"I wish I had magic," the little girl said. "Just a little bit. Then I could run and no one would know. I'd make myself invisible and no one would see me."

Solanda looked out the window, knowing her expression was too sympathetic for a cat. There was a ring of oaks at the edge of the lawn. They were blowing in the breeze. Maybe there would be another storm. Maybe this storm would finally cool the place off, although she doubted it. Nye's hot season was the worst she had encountered in any country she had ever been in.

"Esmerelda!" her mother's voice echoed from the hallway. "Why is your door closed?"

Esmerelda gasped and pulled down the window so quickly she almost caught Solanda's tail in it. Then she leaped onto the bed, stretching out. Solanda jumped beside her and curled up at her feet just as Esmerelda's mother opened the door.

The woman's face was flushed. She looked like a tomato about to burst. She was so tightly corseted that her body looked flat, and Solanda wondered how the woman could even breathe. She wore an evening dress of white satin that accented the redness of her face. The sides were lined with sweat.

"What are you doing?" she asked. Then she frowned. "How did that mangy cat get in here?"

Solanda growled softly in the back of her throat. She was not mangy. And the woman had never called her that before.

"I told you that you were supposed to be in here by yourself to think about what you did today. Things could have been much worse. Fortunately, she was in good mood. You know what those people can do? Why it's said they can cut the skin off a person with the flick of —"

Solanda yowled, and the woman stepped back, a hand over her heart. Esmerelda sat up, worry on her small face.

"Are you okay, Goldie?"

Solanda licked her right paw as if she had twisted it. She was not going to let that woman tell this little girl about Fey atrocities — even if they were true.

"Come on, Goldie," Esmerelda's mother said. "There's some beef for you in the kitchen."

Usually that would have gotten Solanda off the bed. But she could sneak down after everyone was asleep and take what she needed. Right now, she wanted to stay beside Esmerelda.

"Goldie," the woman said.

Esmerelda, good child that she was, bit her lower lip and said nothing. She didn't beg for the company that she obviously wanted.

"Goldie!" her mother sounded exasperated now. Then she shook her head. "Why do we put up with this animal?"

Neither Solanda nor Esmerelda answered.

Finally Esmerelda's mother sighed. "All right, she can stay. But I do expect you to sleep in that dress tonight and to think about how you could have hurt us all. That rip should be a reminder of the danger your misbehavior put us in. Nye isn't the place it used to be, child. Do something wrong, and those Fey will harm all of us."

Then she pulled the door closed, and Solanda heard the boards creak as she made her way down the stairs.

Esmerelda's fingers played with the rip. Solanda looked at it, then crossed the bed, took the skirt in her teeth and pulled. The rip grew. Esmerelda giggled, then covered her mouth. Solanda pulled harder. If the little girl had to sleep in these clothes, she might as well be comfortable.

Esmerelda ripped the pantaloons too, along the dirt line, giggling as she did so. "Mommy will think I did it when I was running," she said. "You're so smart, Goldie."

Of course she was. Solanda preened and allowed herself to be petted one more time.

Then Esmerelda looked at the door, her smile fading. "Sometimes I think Mommy doesn't want me. She wants somebody else. Somebody perfect."

Too bad she didn't realize that the child she had was better than perfect. Solanda sighed softly. Some people had more than they deserved.

3

The idea came to her in the middle of the night, in that hot and stuffy room. She could take Esmerelda away, and Esmerelda's parents wouldn't even know it had happened. But it would take the cooperation of the Fey Domestics.

Fey magic was divided into two parts: warrior and domestic. Warrior magic was designed for warfare. Some Fey magic turned its practitioner into a weapon, like the Foot Soldiers who had fingernails that could slice better than a blade. Domestic magic could not be used to fight any war. Domestics lost their magic if they killed. Their magics were healing magics or home-bound magics, such as spells that made chairs more inviting or fires warmer.

The next morning, after making certain that Esmerelda got breakfast, Solanda slipped out the cat door. She went to the Domicile that the Fey Domestics had set up just outside of town. The Domicile had been built especially for the Domestics, and covered with various protection and healing spells. It was a traditional U-shaped building — with hearth and home magics in one length of the U, the healing wards in the other, and the middle section as a meeting place in between.

Solanda usually didn't seek out the Domestics. They always wanted to experiment with her — have her try on a new cloak covered with some sort of rain protection or have her taste a new food to see if it had an effect on her Shifting. The last time she had been in a Domicile had been when she had broken a paw jumping from a tree in one of the last Nye battles. The Domestics had mended the bone, and had given her a smelly ointment she had to apply in cat form. She had thought the stench alone would kill her.

As she mounted the steps to the center part of the building, she shook off her paws. Here she would not Shift to Fey form. The Domestics weren't as obsessed with power as Rugar was, so she didn't have to use her height as a reminder of the strength of her magic.

She pushed open the door and stepped inside.

The air was cool and welcoming. It smelled of a sea breeze. Bits of magic floated in the air. Spinner's magic. They were working on their looms. She could hear the hum just down the corridor.

A Baker entered, his fingers dusted with flour. They glowed. And she knew he had spelled the bread he'd been baking to remain fresh for as long as possible. It was a traveling spell, one most often used when troops were heading off to battle. She wondered if someone had requested it.

"I'm here to see Chadn."

The Baker nodded, then slipped through a door that led to the Healing part of the Domicile. Solanda hopped onto a chair. Her mood rose and she cursed, jumping down. She didn't need to be spelled, to wait, happy and contented, on a chair dusted with Domestic magic. Instead she paced the cool floor and wondered why she couldn't smell the baking bread.

Finally Chadn entered the room. She was a young Shaman, although the toll of her power had already turned her hair white. Her face was wizened, her mouth a small oval amid wrinkles. Only her eyes were bright — sparkling black circles of light in a ruined face.

She had been assigned to stay with Rugar during the war and she was happy to be free of him. Shaman were the most independent Fey: their Vision as strong as those of the Leaders, but their magic Domestic so they could not rule a warrior people. They were the wise ones, the advisors, supposedly the strength behind the Black Throne. The Black King required a Shaman of his son, but did not use one himself. He had dismissed his own, years ago, for disobeying him. It was one of many areas where the Black King broke with tradition.

"Solanda," Chadn said. "I had hoped to see you."

Solanda jumped on an end table and was relieved that her mood did not change. She sat on her haunches and looked into Chadn's face.

"I have a request," she said. "It's for a Nyeian child."

"A child?" Chadn sounded surprised. "Not a Fey child?"

Solanda shook her head.

"I had Seen you with a Fey child."

The Shaman's Visions — and the Vision that leaders like the Black King had — allowed them glimpses into the future. Some said that the glimpses allowed the Visionary to change the future. Others believed that the glimpses led the Visionary to that future.

Solanda's eyes narrowed. "I have not been with a Fey child."

Chadn nodded. "It was on Blue Isle. The child was a Shifter, and you kept her from death."

Solanda's whiskers twitched. "I told Rugar I would not go to Blue Isle with him."

"The future of our people lies with you, Solanda."

"And a child?" Solanda raised her chin. "Are you sure it was a Fey child?"

"Not entirely," Chadn said. "The child had blue eyes."

Solanda gave a soft grunt of surprise. She had heard of blue-eyed people, but she had never seen one. "The child couldn't be Nyeian?"

"She was Fey, and newborn. She had a birthmark on her chin. Only her eyes were strange, and perhaps that was because of the Shifting. I Saw you put your hands on her lips, and swear to protect her, raise her, and make her strong. Then I Saw her full grown, saying you had been the closest thing she had to a mother."

Solanda laughed, although inside she felt cold. A Shifter only swore to protect a child who held the future of the Empire. A blue-eyed child that Shifted? The center of the Empire?

"Visions can be altered," Solanda said. "I am not leaving Nye."

"You may have no choice."

"I'll always have a choice," Solanda said.

Chadn inclined her head toward Solanda as if giving in on that point. "What does the Nyeian child need?"

Solanda took a deep breath. "She is different from any other Nyeian I've seen. Strong, independent. She met Jewel yesterday and is being punished for it. I would like to remove the child from her family and bring her here, to be raised among us. She will be useful when she's grown. She will be part of the second-generation, the Nyeians that rule Nye for the Fey."

Chadn stared at her for a moment. "So take her. Shifters steal children."

"This one's mother will raise a fuss if she's gone."

"What mother wouldn't?"

"She'll come to us."

"And you can't prove to the Black King that we must keep the child."

"Not yet, anyway," Solanda said.

Chadn folded her hands over her stomach. "You want a Changeling."

"Yes," Solanda said.

"How old is the child?"

"Five."

Chadn sighed. "Have you asked the child if she's willing to leave?"

"Not yet. I wanted to know if I have help first."

"You will keep the child at your side?"

Solanda frowned. That wasn't a normal request. Shifters rarely kept children. They usually brought them to Domestics to raise. "Must I?"

"At five, it will be you she trusts."

Solanda shrugged. "Then she shall stay with me."

"And you will stay away from Blue Isle." Chadn said that not as a question, but as a statement.

"Rugar will not let a Nyeian child in his war party."

"So the child serves two purposes." Chadn's eyes narrowed. "Has she magic?"

"Of course not." Solanda laughed. "There is not magic outside the Fey."

Chadn frowned. "I am no longer certain of that."

"Because you Saw a blue-eyed Shifter?"

"Because I Saw a great war, coming when we least expect it."

"War is part of Fey life." Solanda jumped off the table and headed for the door. "I'll bring you news of the child tomorrow."

"I'll have Changeling stone ready," Chadn said. "But realize before you act, that this is for life."

"I already know that," Solanda said. "I have chosen well."

"I hope so," Chadn said.

4

olanda went to the docks and sat on a fence. She loved it here. The Infrin Sea formed the most natural harbor on Galinas, and there was always some sort of activity. Toward the north end of the harbor, the Nyeian builders made the great ships. Those ships traveled all over the known world, and now Fey Domestics helped unload cargo that would go all over the Empire.

Ships from Blue Isle had stopped coming to Nye when news reached them of the Fey takeover. She would never see an Islander, never learn more about them than she already had.

And that would be all right.

For there were some things she couldn't discuss with Rugar's Shaman. Like the prophecies that had been made by another Shaman at Solanda's birth, prophecies that claimed her legacy would be in the children she saved.

Children — not child, like Chadn had seen. Solanda would influence the life of more than one.

The breeze was cooler here, carrying with it the smell of salt and a tinge of dead fish. That smell made her stomach rumble. She tried not to think of the things she ate in her cat form, things she would find disgusting when she was in Fey form. Right now, raw dead fish sounded extremely appetizing.

But she didn't go in search of the source of the smell. She had some thinking to do. Prophecies and Visions made her nervous. She had no idea what to do with the information Chadn had given her. Because, at various points in her life, Solanda had been told by Visionaries that her future held contradictory things.

One Shaman had told her she had to avoid the Black Family for she would kill a Black Heir. Another Shaman had told her she would raise a Black Heir. And now Chadn had Seen her swear to protect a blue-eyed Shifter, a newborn who couldn't survive on her own.

Solanda bowed her head. The prophecy she never mentioned, the one her parents had kept silent, had come the day of her birth and she had never forgotten it. The prophecy was a cold one: she would die before her time, far from home, for a crime she did not regret.

The Fey did not believe in crime. They were constantly at war, so the crimes that plagued other races — murder, theft — were absorbed into the wars themselves. The Fey only punished two crimes: treason and failure. Both of those crimes were considered crimes against the Empire. Failure was a large crime, encompassing the failure to follow an order, or the failure to defeat an enemy in a prolonged battle.

Treason was any crime against the Black Family and was such a heresy, that it wasn't even discussed among rational Fey.

Both crimes bore the penalty of death.

It seemed to her that she would never commit crimes like that, that the prophecies had come because she was a Shifter, not because of her character. She wasn't as flighty or as difficult as anyone said she was.

And besides, she had to take care of Esmerelda.

She wished she could be there the morning that Esmerelda's parents discovered the Changeling. It would look like Esmerelda, even act like her — if stone could act like a living breathing creature. But it would only last a few days, and then it would cease to exist. They would think Esmerelda dead, when, in actuality, she was only gone.

Then, perhaps, that wretch of a mother would regret how she treated her daughter.

Esmerelda would live a life she couldn't even imagine now. She wouldn't have to wear six layers of clothes on the hottest day of the year, and she would learn how to live life to its fullest instead of remaining indoors and studying all the time.

Esmerelda would be the closest thing to Fey that a Nyeian could be — and for the first time in her young life, she would be happy. Solanda would see to that.

They would both be very happy.

5

olanda returned to the house after dinner. Ultimately, she found she couldn't resist the dead fish that were piled near one of the docks. She had eaten herself sick, and then had to clean every inch of her fur before she even attempted the walk home.

Not that the house was home. In some ways, Esmerelda was.

Solanda used the cat door. Esmerelda's parents were talking softly in the parlor.

"Perhaps boarding school," the mother was saying. "If she is this incorrigible now, imagine what she'll be like when she gets older."

"Give it time, darling," the husband said. "She's still a child. She will learn, as we all did."

"It's just I despair of ever teaching her manners. You didn't see her with that Fey…."

Solanda had heard enough. She hurried up the stairs. She would talk to Esmerelda tonight. Tomorrow the Wisps would come, carrying a bit of stone in their tiny fingers. They'd fly in the open window, leave the stone on the bed and it would mold itself into a replica of Esmerelda while Solanda was leading the real Esmerelda out of the house.

Quick, neat, and completely perfect. The parents wouldn't have to worry about manners or boarding school. Esmerelda would get her heart's desire. And Solanda would have her reason for staying in Nye.

The door to Esmerelda's room was open. Esmerelda sat beneath a lamp, a long skirt over her lap. The air was stuffier than usual, and Solanda saw that the window was closed.

It had probably been closed all day. Sunlight had poured in, and the poor child had had to sit in the heat, working on some task her mother assigned her.

When Solanda got close, she saw what it was. The child was attempting to mend her own ripped dress.

The stitches were uneven, and Esmerelda had stitched the bottom layer of fabric onto the top. That would make her mother even angrier. Esmerelda's eyelashes were stuck together, her nose was red, and there were tearstains along her cheeks.

"Goldie!" she said, and let the dress topple to the floor. She was wearing another dress, equally inappropriate to the hot weather. She reached for Solanda, but Solanda jumped onto the windowsill.

She was not going to be hugged by a hot sweaty child — not, at least, until the window was open and the fresh air came inside.

Esmerelda glanced toward the door. She put a finger to her lips, as if she thought Solanda were going to give her away, and then called, "Mommy! Can I go to sleep now?"

Solanda froze in her spot. She didn't want to be seen in here, not tonight. She wanted to have her conversation with Esmerelda in private.

"Are you done with your dress, darling?"

"Yes."

Solanda looked at it. The dress was ruined. The poor girl would have an even more difficult day than usual tomorrow.

"Then blow out the lamp. Good night."

"Good night." Esmerelda pushed the door closed. Then she went over to the window and opened it.

A strong breeze came in, and on it, Solanda smelled rain. Maybe, after she spoke to Esmerelda, she would go outside. By then it would be raining, and she would be able to cool down.

Esmerelda put her hand over the lamp's chimney and blew. The flame inside the glass went out. Solanda blinked in the darkness, letting her eyes adjust. It only took a moment. There were clouds over the moon this night, and it was very dark.

Esmerelda went back to her chair. "I wish you knew how to sew, Goldie."

"I don't," Solanda said. "But I know someone who does."

Esmerelda let out a small yelp, and put her hands over her mouth. She peered around the room as if looking for the source of the voice.

Solanda had to go slowly with this. The child wasn't used to magic, not like Fey children were.

"I could take the dress to her tonight," Solanda said, "and by morning, you wouldn't even know there had been a rip in it."

Esmerelda's eyes were wide. She finally turned in Solanda's direction. "You can talk, Goldie?"

"As well as I can listen." Solanda jumped from the windowsill to the bed. The room had cooled down. The fresh air felt marvelous. "What would you think, Esmerelda, if I took you to a place where you could wear comfortable clothes, play with children your own age, run and jump and swim to your heart's content? What if I told you that you would never have to sew another stitch, have another music lesson, or sit in a corner when you've done something that your mother didn't like."

Esmerelda looked for her, but clearly didn't see her. Cat's eyes were far superior in the dark. Solanda watched the child lick her lips, rub her hand over her knees, and then sigh.

"How long would I stay?" Esmerelda asked.

"Forever," Solanda said.

"Would I have to be a cat?"

Solanda laughed. For all her verbal sophistication, Esmerelda was still a child at heart. "No," Solanda said. "You'll stay just as you are."

"Would Mommy come?"

"No."

"Daddy?"

"No."

Esmerelda's shoulders stiffened. Her little body looked rigid. "Who would love me then?"

Solanda started. She hadn't expected that question. "I would be with you," she said.

Esmerelda was silent, as if she were thinking this over. "Where would you take me?"

"To my people," Solanda said.

"I'd live with cats?"

"No," she said gently. "With the Fey."

Esmerelda gasped. She held onto her chair as if she expected to be dragged from it.

Solanda wondered if she should have said that, but she had never taken a child before. Certainly she knew of no one who had ever taken a child of this age.

But Chadn had said she had had to speak with the child, and the choice to come had to be the child's. There was sense in that. Esmerelda, at age five, would always have a memory of living with her parents. She needed a memory of her choice to leave them.

"Esmerelda," Solanda said. "I—"

"No!" Esmerelda screamed. "No!"

She launched herself out of her chair as if her voice had given the ability to move again.

"Help! Mommy! Help!"

Solanda's ears went back. She hadn't expected this from Esmerelda, not her sane, different child.

"Esmerelda, I only want to give you a better life—"

"Mommy! Daddy! Help!"

Finally Esmerelda pulled the door open and blundered into the hallway. Solanda followed, tail between her legs, ears still back. The little girl's screams echoed down the stairs. Her parents had reached her, and they both put their arms around her. Esmerelda was too terrified to be coherent.

Then the mother looked up the stairs. She saw Solanda, her gaze flat.

And Solanda realized she had no choice.

She Shifted, her body lengthening, her tail disappearing, her fur becoming skin.

Then she walked, naked, to the floor below.

Esmerelda's mother gathered her child in her arms and backed away. The father placed himself in front of his small family, arms out.

"You came from the Black King, didn't you?" the woman said. "To punish us by stealing our child."

"It's not about you," Solanda said.

Esmerelda peeked around her father, eyes wide. Solanda had never, in her entire life, been so conscious of her nakedness.

"Wh-what do you want?" the father asked. He was trying to sound brave. Like most Nyeians, he was failing.

"I had hoped to take your daughter, but it seems that she prefers this place, even though you treat her as less than house pet. It seems, for reasons I cannot understand, that she loves you."

"Of course she does," the woman said. "We're her parents."

"As if that's a divine right." Solanda stopped on the middle stair.

The family cringed below her as if they expected her to strike them with a lightning bolt. She didn't have that kind of magic. They had seen the extent of her powers, but apparently they didn't know that.

"She is a child," Solanda said. "She is to run and play. She is to have friends of her own age. She is to have comfortable clothing so that she can move without tripping. She is supposed to get dirty, to rip her skirts, and fall on her behind. She is to have some joy in her life. Do you understand?"

"I thought you Fey were supposed to leave us alone," the mother said. "I thought —"

"Be quiet," the father said.

Esmerelda clung to her father, her curiosity moving her closer.

"You will give her those things," Solanda said, "or I will take her from you. Do you understand?"

"Yes," the father said.

"You can't do this," the mother said. "You can't change our customs. The Black King promised you wouldn't."

"A promise made to a conquered people is worth nothing," Solanda snapped. "You will do what I say, or the child is mine."

"Mommy." Esmerelda reached for her mother. Solanda's eyes narrowed. Couldn't she see that her mother saw her only as a thing to be trained, to be forced into the right and proper life?

Probably not. It was too sophisticated a concept for her. The same innocence that allowed Esmerelda to accept a cat's speech, allowed her to believe that she was loved.

"Do I take her now?" Solanda asked.

"No," the father said. "We'll do as you say."

"But our friends —"

"Shut up," the father snapped. "Do you want to lose her?"

For a moment, the mother's gaze met Solanda's and in it, Solanda saw something she recognized, a coolness perhaps, a calculation. How would that woman have answered if she had been asked *who would love me then?* Would she have dodged the answer like Solanda had? Or would she have heard it at all?

"She will stay with us," the woman said. She sounded resigned.

Solanda felt a hope she hadn't even known she had die inside her. "Then I'll watch. You will treat that child as if she is more precious than gold. And if you fail, even once, she's mine. Is that clear?"

"Yes," the father said.

But Solanda did not take her gaze from the mother.

"Yes," the woman said.

Esmerelda had stepped to her father's side. She was still holding his leg. "Are you Goldie?" she asked.

Solanda gave her a small, private smile. "Only for you."

The little girl slipped behind her father again. Her answer was clear, too. She would stay, no matter what. And Solanda had done all she could.

So she Shifted back to her cat form. For a moment, she watched them all, tail twitching, then she ran up the stairs and into Esmerelda's room. She stopped for only a moment, knowing she would never return.

She leapt onto the windowsill, and sighed. She had just lost her excuse for staying on Nye. She was bound to the Black Family. She had to do as they wished.

Rugar wanted her to go to Blue Isle.

Where a Shifter awaited her care. A newborn child, with blue eyes. A child who would think her the closest thing she'd ever had to a mother.

Solanda looked over her shoulder. She heard Esmerelda's voice, high, piping, excited; the soft answers of her parents. Solanda had lied to them. She would not be able to watch.

She hoped they would take good care of her little girl.

Then she jumped out the window, and climbed along a tree branch. Maybe her future had been preordained. Maybe she had no choice. She would raise a Black Heir, maybe kill one, and influence children.

How different would tonight have been if she had told the child that she would love her?

She would never know. Perhaps that was the moment in which everything could have changed. Maybe she had just missed her only chance to save herself.

Destiny is the prequel to Kristine Kathryn Rusch's acclaimed fantasy series about the Fey. Following is a sample from the first book in that series.

Sacrifice

BOOK ONE OF THE FEY

THE VISION

1

The little girl slammed into Jewel at full run, then slid and fell on the wet cobblestone. The girl sat for a moment, her skirts wrapped around her thighs, revealing the pants-like undergarments the Nye-ians insisted on trussing their children in. Jewel hadn't moved. Her hip ached from the impact of the girl's body, but Jewel didn't let the pain show.

She hadn't expected to see a child on the narrow, dark streets of the merchant center of Nye's largest city. The stone buildings towered around the cobblestone road. Even though the sun had appeared after a furious thunderstorm, the streets were just as dark as they had been during the sudden downpour.

"Esmerelda!" A woman's voice, sharp and piercing, echoed on the street. The bypassers didn't seem to notice. They continued about their business, clutching their strange round timepieces as they hurried to their destinations.

The little girl tugged on her ripped skirts and tried to stand. Jewel recognized the look of panic on the child's face. She had felt that herself in the face of her grand-father's wrath. Jewel took two steps toward the girl and crouched, thankful that she was wearing breeches and boots that allowed such freedom of movement. "Why were you running?" Jewel asked in Nye.

"Felt like it," the girl said.

Good answer. Nyeian children didn't play enough. Their parents didn't allow it. The girl had courage.

Jewel extended her hand. The girl stared at it. Jewel's slender fingers and dark skin marked her as Fey, even more than her upswept eyebrows, black hair, and slightly pointed ears.

"Esmerelda!" The woman's voice had an edge of panic.

"She won't like your being dirty," Jewel said.

The little girl's lower lip trembled. She reached for Jewel's hand when a screech resounded behind them. Jewel turned in time to see a woman wearing a dress so tightly corseted it made her appear flat, swing an umbrella as if it were a sword. Jewel stood and grabbed the umbrella by its tip, pulling it from the woman's hand.

"You were about to hit me?" Jewel asked, keeping her tone level but filled with menace.

The woman was a few years older than Jewel, but already her pasty skin had frown lines marring her eyes and mouth. Her pale-brown eyes took in the thin vest that Jewel wore in deference to the heat. "What were you doing to my child?"

"Helping her up. Have you an objection to that?"

The woman glanced at her child. Jewel stood between them. Then the woman bowed her head. Her brown hair had touches of gray. "Forgive me," she said, not at all contrite. "I forgot myself."

"Indeed." Jewel put the tip of the umbrella on the cobblestone and leaned her weight on it. Sturdy thing. It would have made a good weapon, and she had no doubt the woman had used it as such during the recent conflict. "Forget yourself again, and your daughter may lose her mother."

"Is that a threat, mistress?" The woman brought her head up, eyes flashing.

"Mistress." Nye term of respect. The Fey did not believe in such linguistic tricks. There were other ways of keeping inferiors in line. "You're not important enough to threaten, my dear," Jewel said, using the linguistic trick to her own benefit. "I was merely warning you. As a kindness."

She knelt beside the little girl again. The girl's eyes were tearstained. "Don't hurt my mommy," she whispered. "I didn't mean to bump you."

"I know," Jewel said. She adjusted the girl's heavy skirts and helped her to her feet. Then she handed her the umbrella. It was almost as tall as the child. "You just remind your mother that we are no longer your enemies. You have to learn to live with us now."

The mother watched Jewel's every movement. Jewel brushed the dirt off the child's skirts, marveling at the thickness of the fabric. Jewel would suffocate in clothing like that.

"You might also want to let your mother know that pants are more practical for children, male or female."

"I thought you weren't going to change our customs." The woman spoke again, her tone full of bitterness, even though she bowed her head again in the submissive gesture the Fey had commanded. Jewel thought of challenging her on her rudeness but decided the battle wasn't worth her time. She was already late for the meeting with her father.

"We change only the customs that interfere with healthy, productive living. Children are born to move, not mince like some expensive fop at a Nye banquet." Jewel smiled and reached a hand under the woman's chin, bringing her head up so that their gazes met. "She wouldn't have run into me if she had been dressed properly."

"You have no right to change how we live," the woman said.

"We have every right," Jewel said. "We choose to allow you your customs because they keep you productive. You are the one without rights. You lost them six months ago when my grandfather became the leader of Nye."

Finally the panic that had been missing from the woman's face appeared. Her round eyes narrowed and her mouth opened just a bit. "You're the Black King's granddaughter?"

Jewel let her hand fall and resisted the urge to wipe her fingertips on her breeches. "Aren't you lucky I was in a good mood this morning? Threatening me is like threatening all of the Fey at once."

The woman's face flushed with terror. She grabbed the little girl and pulled her close. Jewel ignored the gesture. She took a loose strand of the little girl's brown hair and tucked it behind the girl's ear. "Take good care of your mother, Esmerelda," she said, and continued down the street.

At the corner she glanced back, saw the woman still standing in place, the little girl clutched against her side. Jewel shook her head. The bitterness would get the Nyeians nowhere. They were part of the Fey Empire now. The sooner they all realized it, the better off they would be.

Jewel clasped her hands behind her back. The air was warm and muggy after the storm, except in the shadows of the great buildings. Her grandfather had taken the greatest, the Bank of Nye, and made it his own. Four stories of stone standing like a palace in the merchant section, the building was the closest thing to a palace that the Nyeians had ever made.

The streets were nearly empty for midday. The half-dozen Nyeians gave Jewel a wide berth as they passed her on the street. The Fey guards standing in front of each Fey-occupied building nodded to her as she passed. She nodded in return.

Six months since the Nyeians surrendered, and still her grandfather felt the need for guards. Six months without fighting, and she was growing restless.

Like her father.

He had a plan for the next battle. She was ready, even though her grandfather wasn't sure if the entire force was ready to move again. Her brothers didn't think so, but they were young. The last year of the Nye campaign had been the first time any of the boys had seen battle.

Jewel had fought since she was eleven—nearly seven years—and she had never progressed beyond the Infantry, much to her father's and grandfather's dismay. Her brothers were delighted. They all assumed that her lack of Vision would mean that she would be passed over as heir to her grandfather's throne.

She hadn't told any of them about her strange dreams. She hadn't even visited the Shaman about them.

Finally she arrived at the Bank of Nye. It stood in the center of a cobblestone interchange. Sunlight touched a small corner of the stone, causing it to heat, and steam to rise from the wet. Through an open window she could hear her father's voice mingling with her grandfather's.

They were fighting, just as she knew they would be.

Every time her father mentioned moving beyond Nye, leaving the Galinas continent and heading out to sea, her grandfather objected. The next place to conquer was an island in the middle of the Infrin Sea. Blue Isle had been a major trading partner with Nye. It had also done some business with countries on Leut, the continent to the south. Blue Isle was a gateway that Nye could never be. But it was a gateway that the Black King believed the Fey were not ready to use.

Jewel knew better than to interrupt an argument between her father and her grandfather. Her father had asked her to wait for him, and wait she would. Outside.

Jewel sat on the flagstone steps and propped one booted foot against the wall across from her. She leaned against the cool stone walls, not caring that the roughness of the stone pulled strands of hair from her braid. This was as close as she could get to the open window, but even if she closed her eyes and concentrated, she could not make out the words.

No one else realized the importance of the battle within. Nyeians scurried by, moving as quickly as people could in six layers of clothing, their round faces red and covered with sweat. Jewel had often joked that the Nyeians had lost the war because they didn't know when to take their clothes off.

Not that the wars had hurt business in Nye. The shops were open, and the street vendors hawked wares as if nothing had happened. Fortunately, the bank was on a street filled with other austere stone buildings, a street where no vendors were allowed. She wouldn't have been able to hear anything at all if the vendors had been camped on the cobblestone.

The Nyeians ducked in and out of shops without once glancing at the open, gaily colored flags outside. The flags indicated the type of merchandise—blue for items made in Nye, yellow, green, red, and purple for items made in other countries. The Bank of Nye had transferred its business to the brick building directly across the street, and more than one trader had entered, a money pouch clutched tightly to his hip.

Jewel closed her eyes and a wave of dizziness hit her. The world tilted, and she suddenly felt great searing pain burning into her forehead. Her father shouted, "You've killed her!" and a voice answered in a tongue she did not recognize. Then he shouted, "Someone help her! Please help her!"

Her breath came in ragged gasps. She opened her eyes. A man leaned over her, his eyebrows straight, his hair long and blond. His features were square. He was neither Fey nor Nyeian. His skin was pale without being pasty. He had a rugged, healthy look she had seen only in the Fey, but his features were stronger, as if drawn with a heavy hand. He spoke to her in that strange tongue. *Orma lii,* he said, then repeated a different word over and over.

He cradled her in his arms, holding her with a tenderness she had never felt before. Then the scene shifted. The strange man still held her, but she wore her father's healing cloak.

A Healer slapped a poultice on her forehead. It smelled of redwort and garlic, and stopped the burning from spreading. "She'll live," the Healer said, "but I can promise no more."

"What did she say?" the strange man asked. His Fey had an odd accent.

"That she'll live," her father replied. He was speaking Nye. "And maybe little more."

The strange man pressed her closer. "Jewel." He kissed her softly. "*Ne sneto. Ne sneto.*"

She reached up and touched him with a shaking hand. This night was not how she'd dreamed it would be.

Then the world shifted back. She had moved down two steps, and her forehead tingled with remembered pain. Her throat was dry. A Vision. A real Vision, powerful enough to make her lose her place in the present.

Her heart was pounding rapidly against her chest. She had never heard her father sound so terrified. Nor had she ever seen anyone like that man. His pale skin, straight eyebrows, and blue eyes marked him as not Fey, and his square features and appearance of health meant he wasn't Nyeian. Yet he knew her well enough to cradle her with love.

The bank door slammed open and her father stormed out, his black cloak swirling around his legs. He was among the tallest Fey, and he usually used that height to great effect. Now, though, he seemed even taller than usual.

Jewel had never seen him this angry outside of battle.

She made herself swallow, wishing she had something to ease her sudden thirst. Then she got up slowly, afraid the dizziness from the Vision would return.

"So he said no, huh?" she asked. She had to look up to see his face.

"He said yes." Her father bit out the words as if he resented them.

She frowned. "Then why are you angry? You want to conquer Blue Isle."

Her father looked at her. His eyebrows swept up to his hairline, his eyes fierce. "Because he said I am making a mistake. That I am fighting because I am addicted to slaughter, not because I want to add to the Empire. He said it would be good for me to die on the battlefield so that I don't bring that taste for death to the chair of the Black King."

Harsh words. Too harsh. The fight between the men must have been deep. "He was speaking in anger," she said.

"He believed it was truth." Her father stomped down four stairs, then stopped. At this vantage she was as tall as he was. "No matter what he says, I am taking you with me."

"What about my brothers?" Jewel asked. The last time her father had taken her on a campaign, he had done so that she might care for the boys.

"They're too young for this trip. Meet me in my quarters tonight and bring the Warders. We have a campaign to plan."

He turned his back on her and continued down the stairs. When he reached the street, the Nyeians backed away from him. He hurried across the cobblestone, his cloak fluttering behind him.

Jewel braced one hand against the wall. The dizziness was gone, but a disquiet had settled into the pit of her stomach. She had had her Vision after her father had decided to go to Blue Isle. Were the two connected?

She shook her head. She knew better than to make such speculation about Visions. They existed to guide leaders. She should be happy she had a Vision of such strength. It settled a fear that she would never have the power to be Black Queen.

In spite of herself she felt an odd joy. Her father would take her on her first real campaign—not as a soldier and caretaker for children, but as a leader. One who would help plan.

No matter what her grandfather said about settling, he was wrong about one thing: the fight was in their blood. The restlessness she had felt for the last six months would be put to good use.

She pushed herself away from the clammy stone wall. The face from her Vision rose in her memory.

"Orma lii," she whispered, even though she didn't know what it meant. She was going to face her destiny as a Fey should, in full battle gear, weapons drawn.

THE BATTLE
(Nine Months Later)

2

The thick, heavy clouds made the afternoon as dark as night. The rain fell in sheets, the huge drops thudding as they pummeled the muddy ground. Nicholas's hair was plastered to his face. A moment outside and he was soaked. No one had seen him step into the courtyard. Lord knew what kind of trouble he would get into for going out into the rain.

The servants had to protect the young Prince from himself, at all costs. Even if he didn't want the protection. He was eighteen, more than old enough to make his own decisions.

His hand brushed the hilt of his sword. The sheath was tied to his leg, the leather thongs chafing against his skin. The jeweled hilt was slick. Fighting in such conditions would be dangerous, but he welcomed the challenge.

The courtyard was empty except for a thin cat running for shelter. The stable doors were closed, and lights burned inside. The grooms were working with the horses. The servants' quarters were mostly dark, except for Stephen's cabin up front.

Stephen was an old man who had served as sword-master for the royal family. He had taught Nicholas's father to use the sword decades ago and then had had no duties until Nicholas had turned fifteen. During those years Stephen had become a scholar, studying the history of Blue Isle. He had also become an expert in Nye culture, then had turned his attention to what he called the next threat: the Fey.

Nicholas didn't care what kind of threats he faced as long as he learned to fight. Stephen had been teaching Nicholas for three years now, and though Nicholas had become proficient, he still couldn't beat his swordmaster.

The shutters were closed, but a light burned within. Nicholas knocked. He heard a chair scrape against wood, and the bolt go back before the door swung open.

The flickering candlelight added depth to Stephen's wrinkles. His short gray hair was tousled. He was wearing his winter sweater and a pair of heavy pants, even though it was the middle of summer. "By the Sword," he said. "You're drenched. Get inside before you catch your death."

Nicholas pushed the hair off his face. His hands were red with cold. "No," he said. "Come out. We have practice."

"Not in this weather, we don't," Stephen said.

"I have to learn to fight in all conditions," Nicholas said.

"But I don't have to teach you unless the sun is shining. Now, come in and dry off."

Nicholas stepped inside. Stephen was the only servant who could speak to him with such disrespect, probably because Stephen was the only one whom Nicholas actually trusted.

The air inside was warm. A fire burned in the fireplace, and a book was open on the table. Stephen kept his quarters spare but comfortable. "What were you thinking?" Stephen asked. "You know we never fight in such weather."

"It's been three days," Nicholas said. "I'm tired of being inside."

"You'll be inside until the storm breaks."

"But we don't know how long that will be. It never rains like this in summer."

"I know." Somehow Stephen made the two words sound ominous.

Even though Nicholas longed to warm up near the fire, he wouldn't let himself go any farther without Stephen's invitation. Stephen had only so much space in his single room. He filled it with the table, three chairs, an end table, and a pallet on the floor. A wardrobe stood against one wall. The others were decorated with swords and knives, all different shapes and sizes. Stephen claimed they had once been used in battle, but Nicholas doubted that. Blue Isle had never seen much fighting— even the Peasant Uprising wasn't a real war, according to the Nyeians who visited the palace. Nicholas liked to think that Stephen made up the stories of battles to give himself a purpose. After all, the King really didn't need a swordmaster. Nicholas was learning the art because anything was better than spending his days in a room with Auds.

"Come on in," Stephen said. "I'll give you some mead."

Warm mead sounded good. Nicholas removed his dripping coat and hung it on the peg behind the door. He shook the water from his long hair like one of the kitchen dogs. Stephen sputtered as he was sprayed, and wiped his face.

"They should have an etiquette master for young Princes," Stephen mumbled.

"Sorry." Nicholas grinned. He could never have done anything like that in the palace. Someone would see and report back to his father. Nicholas never quite measured up to his father's wishes. His father wanted Nicholas to be a scholar, to know all he needed to know about the realm. Nicholas wanted to ride horses and win sword fights, and impress women—if only he knew any women to impress.

Stephen went to the fireplace, grabbed a stone mug from the rack on the side, and dipped it into the pot of mead warming at the edge of the fire. He used a cloth to wipe off the end.

Nicholas took the mug, then took a sip. The burning-hot liquid coursed through him, warming him as it went. He liked Stephen's mead. It was sweet, as mead should be, but Stephen always added butter, which he stole from the buttery. It made his mead so much richer than the King's.

Stephen closed his book, then sat at the table. He kicked out a chair, which Nicholas caught with his free hand. Nicholas sighed. "I guess this means we aren't going out."

"I am an old man," Stephen said. "I believe in guarding my health."

"Then maybe we could do some close maneuvers inside. I'm still not as good with a dagger as I would like."

Stephen grinned and glanced around the room. "I value my possessions," he said.

Nicholas did not grin back. He wasn't sure if Stephen had insulted his progress or not.

"And you are doing just fine with a dagger." Stephen rested his arm on the closed book, his hand clutching his own mug. "I think now you are a match for any swordsman who would challenge you."

"Even someone from Nye?"

"Anyone," Stephen said with the same solemnity he had used before.

Cold water dripped off the tips of Nicholas's hair onto his wrists. He adjusted his position so the drops ran down his back. "You really think I'm that good?"

"I think so. Now it's only a matter of practice."

"Great," Nicholas said. He took another sip of mead. He had never expected to receive Stephen's full approval. But Stephen was acting oddly today. "Something's bothering you, isn't it?"

"The weather," Stephen said. "I have lived in Jahn most of my life. I have never seen summer rains like this."

Nicholas shrugged. "Things change."

"That's what I'm afraid of," Stephen murmured.

"What do you mean?"

Stephen shook his head. "An old man's wanderings on dismal summer days. When the sun returns, I will be myself again."

"I hope it comes back soon," Nicholas said. "I am getting restless."

Stephen smiled. He set his mug down, the muscles rippling in his thick arm. "You wouldn't be if you studied as you were supposed to."

Nicholas grimaced. He glanced at the single, shuttered window, then at the glow of the fire. The heat was pleasant, although he was shivering from his wet clothes. He hated the lights in the middle of the day, and he hated to be restricted. Sometimes he worried that all of his practice, all of his work, would fade away. He would lose his skill because the rain forced him indoors for days.

"I am too young to spend the rest of my life in a room," Nicholas said. "Besides, my father isn't that old. He'll live a long time. I won't become King until I'm older than you."

Stephen raised a grizzled eyebrow. "Older than me." His tone was flat, as if the choice of phrasing had bothered him. He leaned back, tilting his chair on two legs, and frowned at Nicholas. "Have you ever thought that your father might need an adviser?"

"My father has a hundred advisers."

"All with their own agendas and concerns. You would be the only one who would share his concerns."

"Me?" Nicholas took another sip of mead. The liquid had cooled and was thick and sugary. "He would never listen to me."

"On the contrary," Stephen said. "I think he would welcome your advice."

Nicholas stood and paced around the small room, leaving boot prints on the wooden floor. He couldn't sit with the thought. His father, listening to him. How very strange. "Has he told you this?"

"Not directly," Stephen said. "Mostly he wishes aloud that you were able to converse with him on several subjects."

Nicholas had heard that, too, and had taken it as nagging. Since Nicholas's mother had died, his father had worked as hard as he could to raise the boy well. Even though servants, and later his stepmother, had done the actual work, Nicholas spent some time every day with his father. The affection between them was genuine, but Nicholas had never thought that he could be his father's equal.

"You're just trying to get me to study harder."

Stephen shook his head. "I am just trying to get you to think. Three quarters of swordplay is mental, you know. The more you use that brain of yours, the better horseman and swordsman you'll be."

"I do better when I'm not thinking about what I'm doing," Nicholas said. He stopped beside the fire and let the heat radiate through his wet clothing.

"You do better when you are so practiced, so used to thinking about it, that you put no effort into the thought.

Imagine if you were that way on affairs of state. You are already a better swordsman than your father. You could be a better statesman, too."

Nicholas grinned at Stephen. "You know how competitive I am, and you're using it."

"Yes," Stephen said. He glanced at the shuttered window. The drum of the rain on the roof almost drowned his words. "I think it's time we all do the very best we can."

3

ugar stood on the prow of the ship, his hood down, water pouring down his face. The rain felt cool and good. He had forgotten the feeling of power it gave him to control the weather. The Weather Sprites had done his bidding to perfection.

By morning the rain would break, and the Fey would be scattered throughout Blue Isle.

If the maps, the Navigators, and the captive Nyeian were right.

Rugar pulled his cloak closer. They should have spotted land by now. The year-old charts suggested that the Stone Guardians were near, yet the view was the same: choppy gray water in all directions. The downpour ruined Rugar's visibility, but he had Beast Riders circling—three Gulls, stolen from his father's private force.

Rugar pushed his wet hair off his forehead. His cloak had been spelled to repel moisture, but sometimes he liked the feel of the water on his skin. His bootmaker's magick hadn't been quite so skillful. Rugar's feet were soggy blocks of ice, chafing against the leather. The wind was slight—just enough to push the ships forward without the crew's resorting to oars or spells.

The ship groaned beneath him, the wood creaking as the prow cut through the waves. The steady drum of the rain drowned out the sound of water splashing against the sides. Rugar clasped his hands behind his back. Normally, he liked travel, but sailing was different. Riding from country to country allowed him to fantasize about conquest, but he had never seen Blue Isle, had only heard about it through myths, histories, and the Nyeians, who were notoriously untrustworthy. Rugar's father, the Black King, didn't even believe the common knowledge: that the Islanders had not seen war. But Rugar believed it. Who would attack that Isle? The Islanders had been smart. They had traded with nearby nations, given them favored status even though (the Nyeians said) the Islanders did not need the goods in return. The Isle was completely self-sufficient.

It was also between the Galinas continent and the Leutian continent. The best point from which to launch an attack that would bring the rest of the world into the Fey Empire. The Fey had already overrun three continents since they'd left the Eccrasian Mountains centuries before. They should not stop simply because they'd reached the end of Galinas. It was Fey destiny to continue until all five known continents belonged to the Empire.

The fact that Blue Isle was rich made the idea of conquest all that much sweeter. Within a few days the Fey would own Blue Isle. Rugar would own Blue Isle.

The Black King would apologize for doubting his only son.

A gull cried overhead. Its caw-caw echoed over the rain and the splash of the waves. Rugar looked up to see one of his own men on the gull's back, his lower body subsumed into the gull's form. Only the man's torso and head were visible, looking as if he were actually astride the gull. The gull's own head bent forward slightly to accommodate the unusual configuration, but that was the only concession to the difference. The Rider and the gull had been one being since the Rider had been a child.

Beast Riders were kin to Shape-Shifters, but like a Shape-Shifter, once the alternate form was chosen, the Rider could not be anything else. The Riders chose the time and place for each Shift, but their moods were always governed by the creature they chose to share their Shape with. Rugar did not understand what forced a Riding child to choose a gull instead of, say, a horse. Yet he was grateful that some did; he was getting tired of the complaints of the landed Riders. Those that Shifted into horses had worn their human forms all during the trip. They were pacing belowdecks, threatening that if they didn't return to their equine forms soon, they would lose the ability to do so ever again.

Since Rugar had heard these complaints on every campaign he had ever been on, he ignored them. But in such close quarters, his ability to ignore was growing thin. He now wished he had placed the remaining Riders on one of the other ships, and kept only the gull Riders with him. Even they weren't as useful as he would like. Because of their odd physiology, Beast Riders could travel only short distances in their altered form. Rugar would have loved to have sent the gull Riders all the way to the Isle when the ships had set sail, but that would have killed the Riders if there were no places to land along the way.

Rugar stared straight ahead, as if by concentrating he could make the Stone Guardians appear. No one had spoken to him all day. Since the rains had started, no one had spoken to him at all, except when they needed something from him. He checked on the Warders, as he did every morning, trying to avoid the Nyeian they kept in thrall. So far, everything had gone smoothly.

Just as he had planned.

The gull cried again and dived toward the ship. The Rider held on to the neck feathers with his tiny hands, as if he truly had to balance on the creature. Riders always pretended to Ride, even though they became part of the animal. The gull swooped around Rugar, then landed on the deck, skidding a bit on the wood.

He looked down at the creature. The gull Rider, Muce, let go of the neck feathers, straightened his arms as if they were cramped, and tilted his head until he could see Rugar. Then Muce grinned and slowly grew. As he stretched to his full height, the bird's body slipped inside his own. The gull cried as if in protest. The cry halted as the bird's features flattened against Muce's stomach.

Muce, in fully human form, was taller than Rugar, but had a broadness that seemed almost unformed.

Muce's dark hair, including the hair on his chest, had a feathered quality, and his fingernails were long, like claws. His nose was not tiny, as a Fey nose should be, but long and narrow, hooking over his mouth like a beak. The nose, combined with his dark eyes and swooping brows, gave his face a nonhuman cast.

He was naked, but didn't seem to notice the rain.

"The Guardians are ahead," he said. His voice had a nasal quality. "Beyond them is the Island."

Rugar grinned. "So our schedule is right. We will be there tomorrow."

Muce shrugged. He glanced over his shoulder at the water before them, a furtive, birdlike movement. "From the air it looks as if there are no passages through the Guardians. The water froths, beats against the rocks, and then deadends. I swooped down and saw crevices, but the waves reared at me like live things. I don't think one ship will survive, let alone an entire fleet."

"The Nye had to trade with the Islanders somehow," Rugar said.

"Perhaps there is an easier way. The Nye have no reason to tell us the truth."

"No one lies to the Fey," Rugar said.

Muce shuddered and, Rugar suspected, not from the cold. The Fey had a gift for torture.

"You need to gather the rest of the Gull Riders and see if they can spot a way through those rocks," Rugar said. "The more backup we have, the better off we will be. These ships need to go through intact. The Islanders have never experienced battle. We'll teach them what war really is."

"It sounds like a slaughter," Muce said.

"A morning's worth," Rugar said. "Once they see that they have no way to defeat us, they will capitulate. The Guardians are our only obstacle."

"All right," Muce said, although he sounded doubtful. "I will gather the others and see what we can discover."

Without waiting for a response, he stretched out his arms and slowly shrank to his gull form. The gull, as it appeared from his stomach, finished the cry it had been making when it absorbed. It took a few tiny steps backward before launching itself into the air. Muce grabbed the feathers he had held before and, as he flew away, did not look at Rugar.

The gray skies and thick rain drops obscured the Gull Rider quickly. Rugar watched it go. He clenched his fists. He hoped that what he had said to Muce was the truth. Rugar had had no Visions since the ships had sailed.

He had expected to have a Vision before now. As the ships drew closer to Blue Isle, he had thought the proximity would draw more Visions from him or expand on his last Vision, the one that had brought him there. He had seen Jewel—as a woman fully grown—walking through the palace on Blue Isle as if she belonged there. But that Vision was nearly four months old now, and he had not had another one. For a while he was afraid they were going into this battle Blind. Then he had practiced making tiny Shadowlands, as he used to do as a new

Visionary. The Shadowlands would capture the cups he had placed in the room and conceal them in a space he had made, proving that his powers were fine. On this trip, then, the Mysteries had given him only one Vision to plan with.

He had spoken to no one about his lack of Vision, not even the Shaman who had consented to go on this trip. Visions were unpredictable things. Perhaps, once he was inside the Stone Guardians, he would be able to See Blue Isle clearly.

No one has conquered Blue Isle before. His father's voice rose out of the mist. The Black King's arguments had haunted Rugar since the ships had left Nye.

No one has tried, Rugar had replied, even though he knew he was wrong. The Nyeians told stories from the dawn of their history which told of a force of long boats, twenty strong, that had been turned away from Blue Isle. The stories were so old that some thought them myths.

When his father had learned of that attempt, his protests had become even stronger. The last fight, when the Black King had learned that Rugar was taking Jewel, had been blistering.

She is the only hope for the Empire. His father had leaned on the heavy wooden desk in his office at the former Bank of Nye. *You cannot take her from here.*

I can do as I please, Rugar had said. *She is my daughter.*

And if you fail, what then? If she dies, what will we do? Her brothers are too young, and at their births the Shaman did not predict great things. Jewel will be great—the best Black Queen of all. If you allow her the opportunity to become Queen.

Rugar had taken a step toward his father. I *saw a Vision of Jewel happy on Blue Isle. Have you had any Visions about this trip?*

His father had not replied.

Have you?

A man does not need Visions to know you're making a mistake, the Black King had said. We *need a rest. We're no longer ready to fight.*

So you have seen nothing, Rugar had said. *Nothing at all.*

Rugar took a deep breath. Rain dripped off his nose onto his lips. The water was cool and tasted fresh. Rugar had had the Vision; his father had not. Rulers followed Vision, even if it was someone else's. Rugar had reminded his father of that, even though it had done no good.

He still made this trip without his father's permission.

But permission didn't matter. Rugar had seen Jewel walking the halls of the palace. He knew the history of the Isle. He would fight the easiest battle in the history of his people.

The Fey would own Blue Isle within a day. The Islanders wouldn't even know they had been invaded until it was too late.

4

An unexpected gust of wind blew aside the red-and-gold tapestry of the Peasant Uprising, which his mother the Queen, God rest her soul, had stitched in the second year of her marriage. Rain splattered against the flagstone, and the fire in the hearth flared. The room was small, having once served as a bodyguard's bedchamber, and the dampness added a chill. Alexander shivered in the unnatural cold. He reached over the arm of his chair and gave the faded bell-pull a harsh yank.

The rain was making him cranky. He had overslept that morning, spent the afternoon reading and signing long-winded hand-copied state papers, and eaten his evening meal alone. Now, during his private time, he still had to focus on business. Not even a King turned away an Elder of the Tabernacle. Already Matthias had overstayed his welcome, and he hadn't yet mentioned the reason that he had come to Alexander's suite on this unseasonably gloomy night.

Matthias's blond curls hung in ringlets around his shoulders, and his mustache was damp from steam from his mulled wine. He still wore his vestments for Midnight Sacrament, the long black robe with the bright red sash and the small filigree sword on a chain around his neck. He had removed his biretta and set it on the carved wooden table beside him. The curls on the top of his head had been crushed flat by the weight of the cap.

"Highness," he said with a smile, "you realize you are waking some poor sod from a sound slumber."

"I don't care." Alexander stood and ladled more wine from the small jug hanging over the fire. Near the flames, the flagstones were hot against his leather slippers. "They should have tacked those tapestries well in the first place."

Matthias set his brown mug down and smoothed his robe. "This weather has us all upset, Sire, but that does not mean we must abuse the servants."

Or engage in small talk. But Alexander said nothing. He had long ago learned that if he suffered Matthias in silence, Matthias would figure out that Alexander no longer wanted company.

Alexander hung the ladle in its place beside the hearth. Then he returned to his chair, careful to hold his mug tightly lest it spill. "I do not abuse the servants," Alexander said. "If anything, I treat them too kindly. They run the palace when I should. Unlike the Tabernacle. The Auds go barefoot. Don't accuse me of abusing my servants."

"Auds aren't servants, Sire. By the time they get shoes, they've learned to appreciate them." Matthias stuck out his sandaled feet, still scarred from his years without shoes. "Believe me, they appreciate all the comforts they get."

Alexander sighed. As boys, he and Matthias had been educated together. But Matthias, a second son, was destined to go into the Church. Alexander, an only child, was meant to rule Blue Isle from the moment he was born. Matthias always found a way to remind Alexander of their difference.

"Servants can be disturbed to see to my comfort on a rainy night," Alexander said a bit too harshly.

"Of course they can." Matthias smiled. "But you might want to note that the loose tapestry is the one that depicts the revolt that left your great-grandfather a cripple."

Alexander laughed. Some of the tension flowed from him. The rain was making him melancholy. It reminded him of last winter when his second wife had died, the victim of a spirit that had entered on a chill breeze and had lodged in her lungs.

Alexander missed her more than he cared to admit, even though she had been frail and silent through most of their union. Evenings she sat across from him and allowed him to muse while her needle whispered through cloth. Her tapestries were never as lovely as his mother's, but the subjects were always happier.

Alexander took a sip of the wine. Its spices were heavy, and its warmth muted the alcoholic bite. He preferred mead, its honeyed flavor more to his taste. This night, though, he bowed to his guest's wishes. Matthias couldn't get mulled wine in the Tabernacle.

"Much more of this rain and the crops will rot at the root," Matthias said.

Alexander sighed deeply into his mug. Matthias was neither taking the hint nor getting to the point. Alexander didn't want to run this visit like a meeting of the Council of Lords, but he would if Matthias looked as if he was staying much longer. "It has been raining for only two days," Alexander said.

"But there is water standing in the fields." Matthias leaned back in the chair, his slender form almost buried in the cushions. "I spoke with an Aud this morning who is riding across the Isle on a pilgrimage, and he says every field he passed since Killeny's Bridge looks like a lake."

"Do Auds know what lakes look like?"

"My, you are in a mood." Matthias sipped his wine loudly, and the sound echoed in the room.

Alexander shook his head. "No. I would merely like to relax."

Matthias peered at him over his mug of wine, his blue eyes glinting with humor. "You are being polite this evening? You could have told me that you didn't want visitors. I would have ridden back to the Tabernacle."

"All that way in the rain. I figured I owed you at least one warm drink."

"I am almost through with it." Matthias took another loud sip. He still wasn't getting to the point. The topic, then, had to be one he was reluctant to discuss.

"So," Alexander said, deciding to force Matthias to leave. "You did not abandon your warm room on a night like this to discuss crops with me. Tell me about Nicholas. That's why you're here, isn't it?"

Matthias nodded and cupped his mug between his hands. "Your son, Sire, has the heart of a warrior. He arrives to class each day with cuts and scars on his fingers. He relishes every wound and would waste the Danites' time describing each if I didn't stop by each morning and cut the conversation short."

Another gust of wind blew in, rattling the tapestry. Where was the damned servant anyway? Alexander would have to make sure the downstairs staff was reprimanded in the morning. "I know that Nicholas enjoys the new physical program. But I want to know if allowing him to fight has improved his study habits."

Matthias sighed. "He does study, Sire, but he argues too much. He claims that religion has no bearing on his future as King."

Faith had no bearing on his future as King. Alexander grabbed his mug, feeling the warmth of the clay against his fingers. He didn't quite know how to explain the study of religion to his son. Without the Rocaanists, Alexander's rule would be twice as hard. Often Alexander and the Council of Lords decided an issue, but the Rocaanists spread the word and enforced the King's bidding through prayer and suggestion of the Church. Nicholas would be an ineffective King if he did not learn the subtleties of the relationship between Church and State.

"I will speak to him," Alexander said.

The door to the chamber opened, and a servant, his gray hair sleep tousled and a tattered brown robe hastily drawn over his breeches, stepped inside and bowed. His feet were bare and red with cold. "'Tis sorry I am, Highness, for me tardiness. The rain has started a flood in the kitchen, and it threatens the hearth fire."

The hearth fire never went out. It was used all night for baking and cooking delicate sauces. It also fed the other fires in the palace.

Alexander nodded. "We have a potential flood of our own. The tapestries need to be nailed more tightly to the windows. The Peasant Uprising is loose and has been dousing us for most of the evening."

"Forgive me, Sire," the servant said, bowing again. "I'll tend to it right away, I will."

He stepped back out the door. Matthias grabbed his biretta and positioned it over the crown of his head. "I think I'd better go, Sire."

Alexander felt a slight, perverse twinge. Much as he wanted to be alone, the fact that he would finally get his wish made him feel lonely. "I'll speak to Nicholas tomorrow."

"Good," Matthias said. He stood, and his slenderness unfolded into uncommon height. Matthias's family had always leaned toward tallness, but Matthias himself would have been considered demon-spawned if he had not shown faith so early. "And I'll let you know if there is a change in his behavior."

The servant entered, carrying a hammer and some wooden nails. Matthias caught the door before it closed and nodded his head slightly, the closest thing he did to a bow. Then he disappeared down the hall. Alexander watched him go. In a way, Nicholas was lucky that Matthias supervised his study. None of the other Elders would have approached Alexander about his son's laxness. A few of the others would have deemed it unimportant, and a few would have used the opportunity, once Nicholas became King, to seize the extra power for themselves. Matthias cared less about power than about preserving the status quo.

The servant pulled aside the loose tapestry, sending more chill air into the room. Alexander stood and wandered next to the fire. He didn't want to catch a chill as his wife had, and if he was going to catch one, it would be now. These rains were unnatural. The summer was usually dotted with rainstorms, but not the constant downpour that the entire Isle was suffering.

"'Tis rotted the wood is, Sire. Whole hunks are breaking away in the wet."

"Then repair it," Alexander said. He didn't care that the silly wood frames his mother had installed to hold the tapestries were rotting any more than he cared that the hearth fire was threatened by a small flood. Something nagged him about this weather. Something more important than small domestic disasters. Something he didn't dare name aloud for fear of inviting the suspicion of the entire Kingdom.

The weather felt unnatural. In all of his thirty-five years, he had never seen the summer sun blotted for days by rain. He wished he could send a man off to Nye to consult with the Seers there, but the Fey had captured Nye in their last campaign across the Galinas continent over a year ago.

The Rocaanists did not believe in second sight, unless it was prophetic vision sanctioned by their God. And there had not been any Rocaanist prophets for nearly five hundred years. Once he had complained of this to Matthias, and Matthias had told him to listen to the still, small voice within.

But the still, small voice within had told Alexander that Kings were not meant to rule alone. He wished he had had enough sense two years earlier to smuggle a Seer back from Nye, so that now he could speak with someone about this fear in his belly, this feeling that the rains were only the beginning of something deeper, something darker, than anything he had ever faced before.

5

The cabin was close and smelled of damp. The tick mattress felt clammy, and the indentation Jewel's body had left when she'd risen in the darkness was still there. She hadn't slept well. She never slept well before a battle. She always imagined herself in the middle of a melee, the smell of blood and fear around her, the ring of swords nearly deafening.

Her father had been right. The Fey lived for battle. Jewel could not keep still for all the excitement running through her.

She had lit her lantern and hung it from the ceiling, where it swayed back and forth with the rhythm of the ship. The light's constant movement made it seem as if the walls themselves were moving. Sometimes she could have sworn they had. In the month since the ship had set sail from Nye, she had grown, and now as she sat on the edge of the bed, her knees brushed the rough-hewn wall. She had to bend as she walked into the cabin, and part of her wished to be sleeping below, with the rest of the Infantry, for she could stand upright in the middle of the hold.

But she wouldn't have to wish much longer. By day-break she would be walking on land again, and she didn't know if she would be sleeping on the cold ground or in her bunk come nightfall. This time she would camp with the Infantry. Her little brothers remained in Nye under her grandfather's care, so she did not have to return to her father's quarters each evening. For the first time she would be a full member of the troop she had been assigned to.

The first time and the last time. When her father learned of her Visions, he would pull her out of the Infantry and he would keep her by his side. She was almost disappointed that she could See. She had been hoping for more battle-worthy skills. Visionaries were leaders, and too valuable to be in the thick of fighting. She had always known that her talents lay in the direction of leadership, but she had hoped she would get fighting skills, like those of a Foot Soldier or even a Spy.

She grabbed her long black hair and swung it over her right shoulder. Then she braided it, quickly and nimbly, wrapped it around her skull, and covered it with an oversize beret. She slipped into breeches, boots, and a leather jerkin. Over that she placed a woolen cape, knitted by one of the Fey's most renowned weavers. The magic woven into the strands repelled liquids, including blood.

She could stay on her bed and wait until the ship made its way through the Stone Guardians. She knew they had been sighted that afternoon. But she would go crazy if she didn't move. Besides, she wanted to be awake to get her first glimpse of Blue Isle, the site of her last campaign.

Then she took the lantern down, opened the glass, and blew out the flame. The darkness was soothing. She set the lantern in its customary position beside the door and let herself out of the cabin.

The deck was slick with rain and sea foam from the unruly waters. She grabbed the wet wooden railing and used it to help her keep her footing. The air was cold and her chill deepened. As she passed the Spell Warder's cabin, she noted light and peered through the portals. They held a Nyeian navigator in thrall. Five of the Warders had circled the Nyeian and were chanting in front of him. They had deepened his trance. His knowledge was critical for this part of their journey. They would not get through the Stone Guardians without the Nyeian's knowledge.

She took the stairs leading up to the prow, where she had last seen her father. He would be planning now and would have no time for her. Still, she wanted to be beside him. She wanted to watch him on his way to his first triumph.

On Nye she had seen the point of the Black King's arguments against fighting. But since the fleet had left, she had come to believe her father more, even though she had not discussed the attack with him. She was a young soldier, having fought only through the last years of the Nye campaign, and she still missed the fighting.

She could only imagine how the career soldiers felt. Most of the Fey fought the wars. The Domestics, while necessary, were never valued. Anyone who lacked fighting skills lacked the heart of a true Fey.

Her grandfather was proposing years, maybe even a generation, without a true battle. The Fey would lose their identities, become as soft and cowardly as the Nye. Her father was right; such a thing should never happen.

When she reached the prow of the ship, she found her father surrounded by some of his lieutenants. The rain was still falling steadily, and she could make out only a few faces in the gloom. Oswel, head of the Foot Soldiers, stood hatless near the railing, his long, slender features bent in a grimace. Caseo, leader of the Spell Warders, was speaking, his cowl down and his hands raised toward the heavens. Her father had his back to her, his head shaking slowly from side to side as he listened.

Jewel approached, walking carefully on the wet deck. She slipped beside her father and put her arm around him. She wasn't supposed to hear the highest-level negotiations: she was a soldier of the lowest rank, a member of the magickless Infantry, often used as advance troops to shock the unwary. But since she was the Black King's granddaughter, no one dared order her away.

Her father's woolen coat was dry, but his hair was plastered against his face. On this trip she had reached his height and had only to look across to him. His lips were chapped, his nose red with cold. Only his eyes were unchanged—black and shiny, their almond shape more appropriate to his hawklike features than to the softer Fey faces. He was of medium height for a Fey—Caseo was taller—but her father seemed to tower over all of them.

He acknowledged her by placing his arm around her waist.

Caseo frowned at her, then glanced at Rugar as if telling him to make her leave. Rugar pulled her closer, his gesture clear. Warders might think they were the most important Fey, but they would get nowhere without the Visionaries. Even Warders were subject to the Black King's family.

The Weather Sprite, Hanouk, was speaking. "We cannot time things exactly, Rugar." The only protection she wore against the rain was a thin chemise. Her ribs and collarbone were visible through her skin, her neck and face so tortured by the elements that she appeared four times older than she was. "You must choose to end the rain early or wait for it to end after we land."

Caseo sighed, the sound barely audible above the thud of the rain. "We can barely see to navigate as it is. Our Nyeian thrall is terrified. Before we placed him under, he swore he could not get us through the Guardians without a current map."

"I was there when he was interrogated. The Nyeian sailed to Blue Isle all his life. He will know the way," her father said.

"His knowledge is over a year old—"

"Besides, he's Nyeian. He could be lying to us," Oswel said.

"No." Caseo's tone was flat. "He will not lie to us. But he may not know if the current has altered or if there have been traps set among the rocks in response to our capture of Nye. This is the most delicate protected harbor in the world, Rugar. One false direction and we will sink."

"We will not sink," her father snapped. His grip around Jewel's waist tightened. "The Islanders are isolated. They believe themselves protected here, and they believe the harbor unnavigable without their petty maps. They know nothing of us or our powers except rumors they may have heard trading with the Nye."

"And we know nothing of them," Oswel said.

"Except that they have not known war for at least ten generations." Jewel adopted her father's tone. "We are a military people. We should be preparing our victory feast instead of speaking of these Islanders with fear."

"The unknown," her father said gently, "is always more dangerous than the known. But Jewel does have a point. We cannot fight with fear." He turned to Hanouk. "We shall arrive under cover of rain and darkness as was the original plan. By the time the ships are in the Shadowlands, the weather shall have cleared."

"I do not like navigating blind," Caseo said. "At least allow the Sailors to do their jobs."

Jewel felt her father stiffen, although the movement was not visible. "You assume that I would place the entire fleet in jeopardy by not placing Sailors at strategic points? Is that what you're saying, Caseo?"

Caseo shoved his hands into the pockets of his robe. Water dripped off the edge of his nose. "I had assumed that you were trusting the Nyeian and the Warders to communicate knowledge to the Navigators. You have said nothing about Sailors."

Jewel bit her lower lip so that she would not respond. She had never heard anyone question her father, but she had never been in a meeting with a Warder before.

"I do not have to approve my plans with any of you," Jewel's father said. "I tell you all what you need to know."

"Then you will be using Sailors—?"

"We have been using Sailors all through the trip, Caseo. Their skills have worked for us for a thousand years. I see no reason to pull them from their posts now." Jewel's father brought his head back, the water beading on his face, making him look fierce. "You may rest assured, Caseo, that I would never rely on the Warders alone."

"You do need the Warders' loyalty for this campaign to work," Caseo said.

"Are you saying that the Warders are not going to be loyal to the Black King?" Jewel's father asked.

"The Black King did not want this mission."

"The Black King funded the fleet."

Hanouk took Caseo's arm. "Arguing with the Black King's son is foolish, Caseo. You have a job as well as the rest of us. Trust Rugar. He is right. The Islanders know nothing of war. We will be feasting in their palace by nightfall."

Caseo kept his gaze on Jewel's father. "Your father always kept me informed on past campaigns."

"I am sure he did," Jewel's father said. "You know everything you need to know now, as well."

The rain thrummed on the wood and water. The riggings groaned, and the ship creaked as it crested a swell. Across from Jewel a rock loomed, going from a shape in the darkness to a menacing presence, its surface shiny with wetness.

"I hope you have asked the Powers to provide a creature of the deep for you," Caseo said, "because if none live in these waters, we shall live and die by our wits alone."

"Our wits," Oswel said softly, "and a Nyeian's memory."

"The Nyeian will help us only once," Caseo said. "We have invaded too deep. He will not have a mind left by morning."

Water leaked behind Jewel's ear and under her cloak. She shuddered. A wave of dizziness hit her. The heavens cleared, and she saw a face looming over her. His eyebrows straight, his hair long and blond. His features were square. *Orma lii,* he said, then repeated a different word over and over. He cradled her in his arms. She smiled at him. His odd look had become familiar.

Her forehead burned. "Are you all right?" her father asked. The pain was greater than any she had felt before. "Jewel?"

A hand tightened around her waist. The darkness returned. The slanting rain was colder, and her father held her against him with such strength, she knew he had been keeping her from falling. The others were staring at her.

"Jewel?" her father asked. "Are you all right?"

She had had another Vision. Or the same Vision. But she deserved her last battle. She wanted it. One more battle, and then she would let him know. Then she would sit at his side as the second heir to the Black Throne.

"I will be glad when this rain ends," she said.

They all laughed, including her father, but the laughter did not reach his eyes. He knew something had happened to her. He would question her about it later. She only hoped he would wait until they had captured Blue Isle.

He turned his attention to the others. "When the rain ends," he said, "Blue Isle will know that the Fey have arrived."

6

✕

*e*very morning the Rocaan would wake before dawn, put on his threadbare Danite robe, and light a single candle. In the thin flickering light, his cluttered chambers would look as spare as the cell he had shared when he was a young Danite awaiting his first assignment, five decades before. He would leave his feet bare despite the swollen joints and aches that had the Elders begging him to see a physician. Then he would cross the thick rug, the pain in his feet easing by the time he reached the stone stairs.

On this morning, rising had been particularly difficult. The rain still pounded the side of the building. His joints hurt him more than usual, and the only way he managed to get himself out of bed was to promise himself an extra pastry at breakfast. It wasn't until he had the candle lit and he was following its tiny light up the stairs that he realized the devotions were no longer enough. The thought pained him. It was a matter he would have to take up with the Holy One.

He opened the door to find the hallway brightly lit. The flames in the covered lamps burned fiercely: someone had just changed the wicks and replenished the oils. These small amenities were growing as his age advanced. It was as if the Elders would protect him from aging through comfort.

The large stones that made up the wall were covered with a whitewash that got repainted each week. The carpet was a thin runner of red woven by the Auds in the Kenniland Marshes. They had used wool specially imported from Nye, wool known for its thickness and softness and complete luxury. Even the lamps spoke of elegance, with their carved gold bases to hold the oil, and their precious glass.

He hurried out of the light toward the back stairs, which he had kept purposely undecorated. The rock was worn smooth from the passage of many feet over the centuries. Its icy coldness was reassuring. He used his left hand to steady himself as he followed the narrow staircase, keeping his right extended before him so that the candle would light his way.

By the time he reached the bottom, the chill had returned the ache to his joints and the blood to his face. Only there did he ever feel alive anymore. It was as if the luxury had bred the yearning soul out of him. He needed the poverty, the hardship, to remember what it was like to believe.

The stairs led to a cramped hallway that was part of the original kirk. This palatial cathedral, the Tabernacle as it was now known, had once been a small saint's cottage holding only an incense burner, an altar, and a kneeling cushion so that the itinerant worshiper could feel closer to his God. The original stone room remained, although three centuries earlier the Thirty-fifth Rocaan had added a window, covered by tapestries, which he used to attack assailants who were trying to eject him from the Tabernacle.

This Rocaan had found the room early in his reign. It had been sealed for generations. He had opened it, cleaned it, and restored it to its former simplicity. Now when he opened the thick wooden door, he found his kneeling cushion, an incense burner, and the small hand-carved altar. He'd had the Elders commission tapestries from the life of the Roca, and then he'd hung a simple silver sword, point down, from the wall, to commemorate Roca's death and subsequent Absorption into the Hand of God.

The room was ice cold and smelled of mildew and seawater. The tapestries were soaking wet and dripping onto the stone floor. A wide puddle ran to his kneeling cushion, and a thin trickle ran from the kneeling cushion to the door.

He sighed. He had designed this room to keep him in touch with the simple faith he'd had as a Danite, and as long as the rain continued, the discomforts of his youth would continue too. When he went up for breakfast, he would ask the Elders to commission new tapestries. The rain would certainly have ended by the time the tapestries were woven.

He stepped around the trickle and placed his candle in its small stand. Then he gritted his teeth and stepped into the puddle.

The water was colder than he'd remembered, and he nearly cried out as the shock ran from his aching feet into his legs. He had to hold up his robe to keep the hem from getting damp. He crossed over to the window and brushed the tapestry aside. The tapestry was so wet that it felt three times thicker than normal. The mildew smell was coming from the fabric.

The rain fell at a slant that coated the side of the building and hit him directly in the face. The darkness was so thick, he couldn't even see the river below. If there was going to be a dawn, it would be rendered invisible by the unnatural clouds. The day before, he had searched the records for any mention of a summer like this one, and never, in all the centuries of documentation, had Blue Isle been subjected to this constant dark, winterlike rain.

Some of the Auds whispered that the Holy One was visiting the rain on Blue Isle as a punishment for the corruption of the Rocaan and the leaders of the Church. But if the Holy One was displeased, He would have been even more displeased by the Rocaan's predecessor, who, the Rocaan believed, was more interested in the wealth of the office than in the people's spiritual well-being.

The traditionalists believed that the rain was the beginning of the final reckoning, that the world would slip further and further into darkness until the Holy One, in His compassion, brought the believers to Him in a final Absorption.

In a meeting the day before, the Rocaan had called together his Elders and asked for their opinion of the matter. Fedo used his knowledge of the Words Written and Unwritten as the basis for his opinion that the rains were merely one of the plagues brought to the Isle to test the believers. Porciluna used his knowledge of the Words Written and Unwritten to determine that the rains were a miracle long promised by God. And Matthias, bless his heretical heart, suggested, with no scholarship at all, that the rains might simply be rains, however unseasonable, inclement, and annoying.

Privately the Rocaan agreed with Matthias. He hated attributing motives to the Deities when common sense dictated something simpler, something rational.

Water ran down his face and stained the front of his robe. He let the soggy tapestry fall back into place. His feet were numb. He slogged through the puddle and stopped at the altar long enough to light his incense; then he knelt on the cushion, wincing as the wet fabric squished beneath his weight.

He bowed his head in meditation, allowing the events of the previous day to flow through him. Once he had believed what all children were taught: that the Holy One heard each still, small voice and carried it with the speed of wind to God's ear. As he grew older, such simple belief was hard to maintain. He had spoken to the Holy One with a still, small voice and with a loud, angry one, and none of his prayers seemed to be answered. Sometimes he thought that the Deities sat in front of the Eternal Flame, Roca cupped in God's Hand, and the Holy One at God's Ear, laughing as they listened to the requests of the poor humans below.

Not a charitable thought for a Rocaan to be sending on the wings of the Holy One to the Heavens above. The Rocaan bent his head and tried again. All these trappings of early faith did not wipe away the years of disillusionment. Even the spicy-sweet smell of raw, cheap incense could not bring back the feeling of joy he had experienced as a Danite preaching the Words Written and Unwritten to the congregations along the Cardidas River.

He wished he could go back and speak to that old woman who had approached him in his first year of ministering. She had come to him after a sunrise service, her face wizened with age, her mouth caved in because of her missing teeth.

You ask us to give our lives to the Holy One, she'd said, her voice quivering, and in return He will give us peace and joy. I have devoted my life to the Holy One since I was a little girl, and I have known no peace and no joy. You must help me, Religious Sir, before I turn my back on the Sword forever.

His words for her then had sounded lame, even to his own ears: You must believe, and the peace and joy will come to you, sister.

Only now he understood her despair. Perhaps no one received peace and joy in this lifetime. Most died before they achieved it, and the very old seemed discontented and angry with life. Or perhaps the Auds and the Elders had misunderstood the Words from the beginning. Perhaps peace and joy came after death. Or perhaps, as he feared in the pit of his soul, peace and joy came only to those Absorbed.

There had not been an Absorption since the Roca.

The chill in his knees had spread through his thighs into his groin. Little shivers ran through him, but he would stay until he felt he had somehow touched the Holy One.

His neck was cramping. Outside, the rain beat harder on the tapestries. Maybe the Officiate who had blessed him as a Danite had been right: We must offer ourselves, failings and all, to the Holy One. The Holy One brings both joy and sorrow to the Ear of God. But you must remember that sorrow is our burden, and God has made no promises to alleviate the pains of the flesh.

The smoke from the incense had grown thick and cloying. The Rocaan coughed, then wiped his hands against his robe. The kneeling cushion was so wet, the dampness was creeping into the fibers of his own garment.

At what point would God allow suffering to end and piety to be achieved? The Rocaan was an old man by any standard. Someday the chill would become permanent, and he would die frail and ill. All men died, and no requests to the Holy One changed that. Even Roca had died in a way, when he'd been Absorbed, all those centuries ago.

He thought he heard voices in the wind, and the creaks and groans of large ships. The Rocaan sighed. Daylight was coming too quickly. He had not yet made peace with his God. The groanings continued, combined with the slap-slap-slap of waves against a hull. Soon he would hear the longshoremen arguing about the best place to pull cargo ashore, and he would no longer be able to concentrate on the still, small voice within.

Longshoremen. The Rocaan paused, thoughts of the Holy One forgotten. He had been speaking with the Elders about the problems with the sea-going community, how half of them were out of work now that the trading with the Nye had ceased. The longshoremen, in particular, were affected.

He stood, his legs shaking beneath the thin, damp robe. The voices were soft, not the usual shouts and curses that interrupted his moments of worship. He gripped the altar to maintain his balance, then waded back to the window and pulled the tapestry aside.

The rain still fell heavily, and within an instant his face was drenched, water dripping down the inside of his robe. The darkness seemed heavier than it had been before. He placed his hands on the wet stone sill and leaned out, gazing upward. He saw nothing more than the individual drops illuminated by his small candle. The clouds were thick. No light could pierce them. The wind was blowing from the west, guiding any ship in the Cardidas to Jahn with great ease. The creaks of the wood were louder now. He looked, but no matter how much he squinted, he could not see any ships or their lanterns.

His hands were growing numb, and he could no longer feel his feet. If there was a ship below, and its captain glanced up, he would see the Rocaan peering out the window like a common schoolboy. Somehow that thought filled the Rocaan with alarm.

He let the tapestry fall, and as he did, he heard a sound he had not heard since he'd been a boy, fishing with his father. The ululating cry of a man signaling to his mates without words. A cry designed to be a call of the wild, although it sounded like no creature the Rocaan had ever heard. Some kind of prearranged signal that required a prearranged action. A cargo ship's captain would not do that.

The Rocaan grabbed his candle and placed it outside the door, careful to set it away from the trickle that had invaded the hall. Then he went back into the room and closed the door after himself, waiting until his eyes adjusted to the blackness before making his way to the window again.

This time he tied the tapestry back and stared at the river below. He heard splashes, and more soft voices, although no matter how hard he concentrated, he could not understand their words. He squinted until finally he could see the outlines of the masts, dozens of them, disappearing into the distance like a ghostly invasion force.

He would have heard had there been a fleet coming to Blue Isle. He would have assigned Auds to minister to their needs, Danites to see to their faith, Officiates to give them contact with the organized Church—and, if they were important enough, an Elder or two to begin political relations. This was different. How different he did not know. He needed the advice of someone else. Someone he could trust. Someone who would look with a clear eye.

He left the tapestry open and went from the room. It felt odd to walk on dead feet. As he bent over to pick up the candle, he noted that his skin was blue. He could not spend any more time in that room this morning. Surely God did not require a man to lose his feet in pursuit of a Blessing. He climbed the stairs, using the wall for support now more than ever, finding that numb feet could not properly judge stair height. When he reached the hallway, he handed his candle to one of the guards.

"Get Elder Matthias for me, and quickly," he said. Then he let himself into his chambers.

As per his instructions, someone had lit his daily fire and placed a tray beside the hearth. He glanced at the warm milk, freshly squeezed from one of the goats housed in the yard, and instead took a small bite of the roll the servants baked every morning. The bread was still hot and doughy in the middle, just the way he liked it. Then he pulled off his robe, leaving it in the middle of the floor, and slipped on the plush red velvet robe of his office, basking in its softness and warmth. He sat on the flagstones and extended his feet toward the fire. A slight needles-and-pins feeling changed almost instantly to deep, agonizing pain as his feet thawed. He grabbed them, startled by the cold flesh on top and the hot flesh on the bottom, and squeezed, as if the pressure would make the pain go away.

At that moment someone knocked on his door.

He sighed; then he backed away from the fire, eased himself into his chair, and put his feet on the ground. He wiped his eyes, swallowed, and, ignoring the pain, called, "Welcome!"

The door opened and Matthias entered, already natty in his pressed black. The robe whispered as he walked. The only concession he had made to the earliness was that he was not wearing his sash or biretta. But his hair was combed and his face already clean shaven.

"I hope, Holy Sir, that nothing amiss has happened," Matthias said, his tone matter-of-fact instead of questioning.

"I certainly hope so as well," the Rocaan said, gritting his teeth. The pain was coming in a steady ache, marred by sharp stabs. "I would like you to go down to my worship room, look out the window, and tell me what you see."

Matthias cocked his head. He was young, the youngest of all the Elders, his skin still unlined and taut. "And what, exactly, am I looking for?"

"I will tell you when you return, since I do not want to influence you. And perhaps, by the time you get down there, what I want you to see will be gone, so do not worry if you fail to see anything at all."

Matthias frowned and clasped his hands in front of his robe. The black robe of an Elder was also made of velvet. The higher authorities in the Church seemed to believe that ranking members should live in comfort. Whenever the Rocaan thought of changing that, he remembered that he would have to give up his soft bed, his morning fire, and his sweets.

Matthias did not look as if he were going to move.

"And one more thing," the Rocaan said, mostly to spur Matthias on, "do not bring a light into the room. I'm afraid you'll have to stumble around in the dark."

"All right." Matthias bowed his head. He backed out of the room slowly.

The Rocaan waited until the door closed before allowing a moan to leave his lips. The pain was easing, but it had been excruciating during his conversation with Matthias. Only the toes continued to hurt. He eased one foot up and massaged it, then the other, noting with pleasure that the blue had left the skin, replaced with healthy red. No toe had an unnatural whiteness, which he had feared. He had seen too many Danites lose flesh to that wintry color.

He took another bite of his roll, then drank some of the milk. Even as the pain left, he felt unsettled. He had not completed his morning ritual. But, if the truth be told, he had not achieved the sense of peace he sought for a long, long time. This intrusion had simply been a little more startling.

He leaned his head back, then heard footsteps in the corridor. They had more urgency than they had had before. The knock, even though he expected it, was sharp and frightening. No vision, then. He had seen ships.

"Come," he said.

Matthias was already halfway into the room. He closed the door tightly, then hurried down the small flight of stairs. "Ships," he said. "I saw ships. Dozens of them. Should I send for the head of the Port Guild?"

The Rocaan rubbed the bridge of his nose with his thumb and forefinger. The pain in his feet was gone, but a headache had started above his eyes. "Before you go, tell me what you saw."

"It took a moment, in the darkness," Matthias said. "That floor is damned wet in there."

"It's the rain," the Rocaan said tiredly.

"Then I saw masts, and if I looked carefully, I saw the ships themselves. They're not Nyeian. I've never seen them before. And it was quiet except for low voices."

"What were they saying?"

"I couldn't make it out."

"Neither could I." The Rocaan let his hand drop. He opened his eyes. Matthias's face was flushed, his eyes sparkling with the excitement. The Rocaan sighed. "I think you must go to the King."

"Holy Sir?"

A thread of irritation ran through the Rocaan. Did he have to explain everything? Matthias was sharp. He should have figured the problem out already. "The ships are unknown, Matthias," the Rocaan said. "They are not planned for. I suspect our visitors are uninvited."

Matthias shook his head. "That's impossible. No one can get to Blue Isle's shores without guidance."

"Someone had to once," the Rocaan said, "or we would not be here."

Matthias took a step backward, then sat in the armchair near the bed as if he needed something to support his weight. "What would anyone want with Blue Isle?"

The question was soft, almost rhetorical, but the Rocaan chose to answer it. "We are one of the richest countries in the world. To ignore us would be foolish."

Matthias looked at the Rocaan, his gaze piercing. "You know who this is."

"I have a suspicion," the Rocaan said. "Nye has shared our waters for centuries and still needed help to arrive at Blue Isle's shores. Occasionally other seafaring folk have tried to come to Blue Isle, only to wreck on the Stone Guardians or be savaged by the current. But there is a group that has never tried to attack us before, and now they hold Nye."

"The Fey," Matthias breathed.

"Just so," the Rocaan said. He sounded calmer than he felt. "And if the tales we have heard are true, they are vicious. You must go to the King, and quickly."

Matthias nodded and stood. He hurried toward the stairs and then stopped. "Even if it is the Fey, we'll be able to defeat them, won't we?"

"With God's help," the Rocaan said. He folded his hands across his bulging stomach. Matthias scurried from the room, apparently satisfied with the Rocaan's answer.

But the Rocaan wasn't. He looked at the closed door. "No, Matthias," he said softly, as if he hadn't answered the question before. "They are soldiers and we are farmers, and we shall be slaughtered before we have a chance to learn how to defend ourselves."

To continue reading this book for free, go to https://www.smashwords.com/books/view/57929 and enter coupon code GB96F.

About the Author

Bestseller Kristine Kathryn Rusch has won or been nominated for every major award in the science fiction and fantasy fields. She has won Hugos for editing *The Magazine of Fantasy & Science Fiction* and for her short fiction. She has also won the *Asimov's SF Magazine* Readers Choice Award six times, as well as the *SF Age* Readers Choice Award, the Locus Award, and the John W. Campbell Award. *Alien Influences*, first published in England, was a finalist for the prestigious Arthur C. Clarke Award. *Io9* said her Retrieval Artist series featured one of the top ten science fiction detectives ever written. She also writes mystery, romance, and mainstream novels, occasionally using the pen names Kristine Grayson and Kris Nelscott. For more information on her work, go to kristinekathrynrusch.com. To find out more about the Fey series, go to wmgpublishing.com.

The Fey Series:

Destiny (A Short Novel)
The Sacrifice
The Changeling
The Rival
The Resistance
Victory
The Black Queen
The Black King

CPSIA information can be obtained
at www.ICGtesting.com
Printed in the USA
LVHW091119050519
616704LV00001B/69/P

9 780615 686158